CW00864772

THE NINTH PRECINCT

A. E. STANFILL

Published 2020 by Gumshoe – A Next Chapter Imprint

Cover art by Cover Mint

1

A RAINY NIGHT

THE RAIN WAS PELTING THE GROUND ON A WARM SUMMER NIGHT, washing. away any signs of murder. Multiple voices along with the sounds of footsteps could be heard in the old part of town, as red and blue lights danced off the side of an abandoned building. A crowd of pedestrians had started to gather, just to get a glimpse of the horrible display that was before them.

"Get these people back, Wilson!" An older gentleman grumbled. He was wearing a gray trench coat with a brown hat, the kind detectives would wear back in the golden days. "This is a crime scene, not a red carpet event."

"Sorry Lieutenant, I have the barricades up," Wilson nervously replied. "You know how people flock to the sight of a murder, it's hard enough just to keep the reporters out."

"Just do your damn job," he flung his arms up in the air before walking over to survey the crime scene. He was aggravated and mad but still had a job to do. What he had noticed first was how gruesome the sight truly was, this time the body was stripped of its clothes, not only that the poor soul had been skinned and nailed to this run down building for the world to see. The lieutenant had witnessed some brutal murders in his time on the force, but nothing to this extent. He pulled his coat tightly around himself and gave a little shiver.

"Doesn't matter how hot it is in the summer, the midnight rain still sends chills throughout the body," a melancholy voice said.

The Lieutenant spun around to see a silhouette of a man standing before him wearing a trench coat quite like his own just of a different color and more, shall you say, modern. "Do you always sneak up behind people?"

He walked up closer to the Lieutenant releasing a cloud of smoke from his mouth and out into the rain, "Keeps a man alive," he joked. "You taught me that."

"That I remember, but I think those cigarettes will kill you first before anyone else gets the chance right, Grant?" The guys laugh sounded like a large bear warning others to stay away.

"Who knows and who cares." He shrugged.

"Cryptic as always. So what brings you this far out of the big city?"

"I was just passing through, seen the crowd and decided to stop."

"Cut the shit," the Lieutenant hissed. "I know you. Dead bodies being hung up in different locations, each one worse than the last. No leads or clues to who the killer could be, this is right up your alley."

Grant took another hit from his cigarette before flicking it to the side, "Guess you figured me out, Harris." He looked at the body nailed to the building, "I was called and offered money from a very wealthy client to help investigate this case."

"Didn't think the money mattered to you."

"It doesn't," Grant said. "I have been looking over this case for some time now, and by the looks of things, the killer is becoming bolder. He must not be getting the attention he's craving. Plus a man has to make a living."

"That means he's become careless." He brushed off the last words Grant said. "The killer will slip up soon enough."

He stepped closer to the body that was on display, "Don't be so sure about that." Grant motioned for him to come closer, "See how perfectly he skinned this person?"

"All I see is a body that got butchered by some crazed psycho," Harris snarled.

"You're not seeing the whole picture here, Lieutenant. The killer sees this as a work of art, this is also the way we have to look at it as well. Whoever this individual is, wants to be seen as an artist, not as a madman." He looked to where the organs should have been. "If you look closely, you will notice how the killer cut the organs out of this body with precision, showing off his handy work."

"Why does any of this matter?"

Grant sighed and lit up another smoke, "These are all clues to finding out the identity of the killer." He exhaled a cloud of smoke, then took another drag from his cigarette.

"How can there be clues? The rain has washed it all away," Harris argued.

"Look closer, Lieutenant." Grant pointed, "Notice how there are markings on certain bones. Not only that, the killer left the mouth open revealing that some of the teeth have been removed. The eyes were left but the eyelids have been cut off. Also, the left ear has been removed, but the right ear has been left alone for a reason. He wanted us to see the earring for a reason. Don't be confused by the body being left out in the rain, it wasn't because he wanted to wash the evidence away. It's because, in his eyes, the victim was a sinner, and he made them into something beautiful. The rain is just a symbol of washing the unclean."

"I see," Harris responded coldly. "Anyways, the coroner is here to take the body. Let's say we go get a drink at the nearest bar. Honestly, the reporters flocking around are starting to piss me off, and you know what that does to me."

"Could need some antacids old timer."

"Any other smartass remarks before we go?" Harris asked as he walked towards his squad car.

"None off the top of my head. Promise me one thing, though."

"What?" Harris's brow raised.

"Once we're done with the drinking, you take me back to the coroner's office so I can take a look at the body again," Grant answered.

"I will see what I can do," Harris replied. Grant nodded turning to take his leave, "Where are you going?"

"To my car."

"Ride with me."

"I will just follow you there," Grant insisted. There was a tone to his voice that told Harris the man he called friend wasn't the talking type like years past.

"Shut up and get in the car," Harris demanded. "Don't forget that you're not a cop anymore, I can still arrest you."

"On what grounds?"

"Disobeying an officer of the law," Harris answered with a grin. "Would you like to get in, or do I need to use the handcuffs?"

He stood there brooding it over, "I will do things your way, for now."

It was a quiet ride to the nearest pub, the only thing breaking the silence was the sound of rain hitting the windshield along with the squeaking of the wiper blades hard at work. There was only one bar that was open at that time of night, and that was good old Willie's. The owner was a good friend of both Grant and Harris's. Plus he was the bartender and enjoyed a good conversation from law enforcement. Thus why keeps his pub open such late hours.

"Lieutenant Harris." Willie smiled. "What can I do you for tonight?"

"The usual." Harris tossed his hat on the bar before taking a seat.

"How about you sir?" Willie looked at Grant and asked.

Grant took off his coat placing it on the back of a chair, "Have I been gone for so long that you've forgotten what I like to drink?"

Willie's eyes widened, "Is that you, Grant?"

"It is, I'm back in town working a case."

The man turned and began pouring a beer for Harris, "Does it have to do with all the strange murders?" he asked, keeping his concentration on the task he was performing.

"You could say that," Grant said as he took a seat.

Willie slid the beer over to Harris before grabbing a shot glass and a bottle of bourbon from behind the counter, "Is that the reason you're back or not?" He poured a shot of liquor and slide it over to him.

Grant grabbed the glass and gulped the drink down, "Another shot if you don't mind."

"Answer my question and the first five shots will be on the house."

Harris could see the glint in the eyes of his friend, and that usually spelt trouble or at least it did in the past. "You know we're not allowed to talk about that case with anyone," he interrupted. "Just let the man have his bourbon."

"Tell you what." Grant held up his glass. "If you give me that bottle, and answer a question for me first. Then I will kindly oblige and give you an answer as well. What do you say?"

"You can't make deals like that!" Harris's voice raised.

"That's where you're wrong, Lieutenant. I'm a private eye now not a cop. The same legalities don't apply to me anymore, if I want to share information to get information then that's what I will do. Or are you not curious about what Willie might know?"

"I was never here, got it?"

"Understood. Do we have a deal or not, Willie?"

Willie set the bottle on the counter, "It's all yours."

"Good, we have an understanding." He began pouring himself another drink. "Tell me Willie, have there been any strange characters hanging around the bar lately?"

"This is a bar? Strange people hang around here all the time."

Grant swallowed down another drink of bourbon, "Let me rephrase that, have you yourself heard or seen anything out of the ordinary?"

"Hmm," Willie ran his fingers through his thinning grey hair. "I haven't seen anything personal, but I've heard stories."

"What kind of stories?"

"Odd ones." Just talking about the things he's heard gave him the creeps, not the kind bar talk he likes.

"Go on." He poured himself another drink.

"Well, I've heard stories of a man dressed in black walking the streets late hours of the night, whistling while carrying a red rose tight in his hands," Willie said with an eerie tone to his voice.

"What does this person look like?"

"Not sure, nobody has seen his face," Willie said.

"Then how do you know if it's a man or a woman?" Harris interrupted.

"How should I know?" Willie responded. "I hear what I hear, but I believe you owe me an answer now."

Grant smiled and pointed towards the other side of the bar, "Looks like that answer will have to wait, you have some more patrons that need their whistles wettened."

"Don't worry the bottle it's on me, but this isn't over." Willie wasn't happy that he was cheated, but he didn't have time to argue the facts for that matter.

"Now that he has gone, I can get to the real reason I brought you here," Harris said.

"I had a feeling you had an ulterior motive for bringing me here."

Harris took another sip of his beer, "Tell me, Why did you leave the force?"

Grant lit up a cigarette and released a cloud of smoke from his mouth, "Reasons." Is all he would say.

"Something must have happened that made you not want to be a cop anymore. You had it all, you went from being a street cop to a detective all in a year. Before you made captain you decided to walk away, there has to be a logical reason to why." Harris seemed like he was hurt in what Grant had done years ago, and wanted some answers.

"If I tell you, you would think that I am mad," he said, drinking down another shot.

"How about you put the bottle to the side and try me."

"No thank you."

Harris shrugged, "At least I tried."

Grant took a drag from his cigarette, "But I will give you this bit of information. I went to an asylum to visit with a man accused of murder twenty-something years ago. His name was Bobby Sikes, after hearing his story I kind of helped him escape to get his revenge on the real killer. That man gave his life to save others. Long story short, when I told my superiors they demanded I keep things hush or I would be demoted. It was then that I made the choice to walk away and become a private eye. Do I question my actions? Do I regret it? Not for a second."

"Did it have anything to do with your brother?"

"It did." Grant nodded. "And I finally found the closure I sought after all these years, not only that my brother's spirit can rest in peace."

"Didn't think you were the religious type," Harris said before taking a drink of his beer.

"Things change when you stare into the eyes of the devil," Grant answered. He pushed the half-empty bottle of bourbon over to the man sitting next to him, "On the house." He stood up and grabbed his coat.

"Where are you going?" Harris asked.

"I said I would have a few drinks and I did. Hell I even gave you some unneeded information." He started to walk away from the table then paused, "Time is wasting, and we need to make a trip to the coroner's office."

Harris looked at his watch, "The place should be empty by now." He slammed the glass on the table, not exactly pleased he was leaving a cold beer behind. "Let's go."

2

THE CORONER'S OFFICE

HARRIS PULLED HIS VEHICLE INTO THE PARKING LOT OF THE CORONER'S office, all the lights on the inside and outside of the building were off. The place was completely enshrouded in darkness and the rain seemed to part, which added more to the already creepy vibe of the place.

"Here we are," Harris said as he turned off the vehicle.

"The place looks closed to me," Grant muttered.

Harris held up a set of keys, "Don't worry about that, I have a way inside." He opened his car door and exited the vehicle, making his way towards the entrance. Grant got out of the car and followed behind Lieutenant Harris, but he couldn't shake the feeling that they were being watched. "Something wrong?" Harris asked, after unlocking the double doors in front of them.

"It's nothing. Let's get inside before it starts pouring down again."

Harris opened the set of doors, "After you." Once inside, the Lieutenant lead him down a dimly lit corridor. There was barely enough light to make heads or tails of what was in front of them, but Grant was used to the darkness, it had become more of an ally than a hindrance to him. "Watch your step," Harris warned. "We don't need to make any unwanted noises, and whatever you do, leave the lights off."

"A little on edge, eh Lieutenant."

"This is no time for jokes," Harris grumbled. "I could lose my job if anyone catches wind of me letting you in here after hours. Think about how that would look if a cop got caught helping out a private investigator."

"I wouldn't let that happen. Besides, you need my help with this case. Let's be honest here, you haven't had any luck and the body count is increasing. These kinds of cases are my specialty, of course my credentials speak for themselves."

Harris stopped at a door that read "morgue" above it, "Your credentials are not in question." He used another key to unlock the door and pushed it open, "I was never here," he whispered before turning his back.

Grant stumbled around the room until he found a small lamp to turn on that gave him just enough light to see. He picked up a clipboard that had a sign in sheet clipped to it, he looked it over thoroughly. "The body has been signed in, but the coroner has yet to look it over. I imagine he or she is waiting until sunrise." He continued to study over the papers until he found what he was looking for, "body was placed on table four, body bag tagged C4."

He put the clipboard back down on the desk and went off to search the room again. It took awhile but he found what he believed was table four when he looked over the body bag his suspicions were confirmed. Grant reached down and unzipped the bag revealing the dead body inside. "If I'm careful the coroner will never know that I examined the body before they did." Leaning his head in closer, he noticed more markings than he had originally seen. Grant took out his notes and began jotting things down.

The eyes being left in place, along with the earring was a the clues he needed to look further into. What really had him concerned was the fact there were no rose petals left behind like the killer had done multiple times before.

This had Grant worried that a copycat killer could be responsible for this pour souls demise. "What's this?" He put a rubber glove on his right hand and reached down to open the victim's mouth, rose petals were stuffed inside, "How did these get here?"

Sounds of footsteps could be heard coming from down the hallway followed by whistling. Grant slowly walked over to the door and peeked his head out, however, there was nobody there. He wanted to call out, but something deep down in his stomach told him otherwise. Instead, he went on the hunt to find out who the uninvited guest that somehow managed to get inside without being noticed. There wasn't a thought in his mind that it could have been his old friend, he wouldn't have allowed that much noise to take place. Question is, where was Harris?

Grant slowly crept down the dark hall making sure not to make any sudden movements that would give him away to the intruder. As he approached the entrance every single light in the building flickered on. Whoever followed us inside must have reset the timer for the lights, Grant thought to himself.

If I don't find Harris and get these lights off we will have some unwanted attention. When he rounded the corner something caught his eye, there was a body lying face down on the floor. "Harris!" Grant gasped, quickly making his way over to his fallen friend, to his relief, Harris had only been knocked unconscious.

"What happened?" Harris asked, holding the back of his head.

"Somebody got the jump on you," Grant replied. "Not only that, this place is lit up brighter than, New York City."

"Damn." He tried to stand straight but was still too woozy and fell back against the wall.

"You should stay here and clear your head," Grant insisted. "Tell me where I need to go, it's not like I can't work a timer."

"Down the hall, fifth room to your left," Harris reached in his pocket to hand Grant the keys, but they were gone. He leaned his head back against the wall and sighed.

“I can tell by the look on your face that something is wrong.”

“Whoever got the jump on me, took the keys.”

"I don't need keys." Grant smirked, "There are other ways of opening a door."

"Just be careful."

"Likewise."

It took Grant all a little time to make it down to the room that controlled the lights to the building. What he didn't expect to find was a flashlight taped to the door along with a note that read, "you're going to need this." He took the flashlight in hand and wiped the sweat from his brow, then slowly entered the room. Grant wasn't afraid of what he would find on the other side, he found himself in worse predicaments than this and survived.

The only thing on his mind was getting the lights turned off, and perhaps a clue to who might be behind all of this madness. Grant turned the flashlight on and looked around the room, to him it looked as though someone had removed the lightbulbs. As he glanced over the room over further he caught a glimpse of a red substance smeared on the wall. Investigating on revealed that it was a drawing of an eye, not just one but many.

Being focused on the wall he didn't notice the cops on the other side of the door. His concentration was interrupted when he heard the sound of metal banging across the floor. By the time he realized what was happening it was too late. Smoke filled the room, Grant's eyes burned and it even hurt to breathe.

Cops wearing gas masks rushed into the room. They had their flashlights and guns in hand aimed at him. "Put your hands in the air!" One of them shouted.

Grant dropped his flashlight making sure to raise his arms up slowly, "Easy guys, this isn't what it looks like." He choked out those words but it did him no good.

Another cop grabbed his arms jerking them down behind his back, slapping cuffs on his wrists, "Shut up and move." He was lead out of the darkroom and back into the hallway where Harris was being looked over by the paramedics. The cop pushed Grant's back against the wall, "Stand here and keep quiet." He pulled the mask off and Grant knew exactly who it was.

"Getting the same treatment from you as always, eh Turner?"

"Shut up!" Turner went to push Grant again.

"That's quite enough from you, Turner," warned the police chief.

"But-"

"I said that was enough!" She snapped.

Turner walked away angry as the chief of police approached, "What do you think you're doing here at the coroner's office at three in the morning, Mr. Dawson?" she hissed.

Instead of answering the question Grant decided to be a smartass, "Me being here of all places got the attention of the police chief. Don't you have a murder to solve instead of worrying about me? Right, Simons?"

"Don't screw with me, Dawson. I can have you thrown in jail for being here."

"You could if I had done something against the law," Grant said. "I know my rights, and seeing how I was helping an officer in need you can't hold me."

Lieutenant Harris walked up holding the back of his head, "He's right Chief, Grant was helping me out of a sticky situation."

She glared daggers at the Lieutenant, "What was Mr. Dawson doing with you in the first place?"

Harris leaned his back up against the wall, "I can't remember exactly."

He closed his eyes. "My head is still aching from whoever got the drop on me."

"Okay Lieutenant, I see what is going on here." Simons snarled, "Get Dawson out of my sight. Oh, and one more thing I expect a full report on my desk as soon as you walk inside the precinct."

"Of course ma'am," Harris replied. "Time for us to be on our way, Grant."

"One second, Harris." Grant looked back at Simons and smirked, "Do you think I can get these cuffs removed first?"

Simons grabbed him by the end of his arm and spun him around, slamming his chest first against the concrete wall, "Someone likes it rough." Grant chuckled.

"You have no idea just how rough I can be." She breathed into his ear. With a turn of a key the handcuffs were off. Simons grabbed him again and shoved him towards Harris, "He's all yours."

"Do you ever know when to leave things alone?" Harris mumbled under his breath as he made his way towards the exit.

"When it comes to Simon's, not a chance."

"Figures." When he pushed open the double doors something fell out of his coat pocket. Grant didn't say anything, he figured the best thing to do would be to pick up whatever object his friend had lost and return it to him once inside the squad car.

He knelt down to find a set of keys lying on the floor, "These are the set of keys to coroners office," he gasped. "Harris said they were stolen from him when he was knocked unconscious. If that was the case, why does he still have them?" Grant felt a nervousness swelling up in the pit of his stomach, it was a feeling he had to quickly shake. Why Harris still had the keys on him doesn't make him a murderer. However, he couldn't let him know of the item he had dropped, not yet anyway.

Grant had barely gotten any sleep the night before, and he stayed up the rest of that morning thumbing through his files on "The Midnight Killer" case in his hotel room. The first file he studied was that of a man named, Leonard Clifton. He was one of those real scumbags that had a rap sheet a mile long. Yes, he liked to throw his weight around with the ladies, on top of that he was known for selling drugs, but did that make him a killer?

The second file was that of a lady that goes by the name, Grace Jones. She had been in and out of an asylum for years now. Having her on file as a possible suspect didn't sit well with him, the killer had already proclaimed to be a male. But still, he had to check all leads just to be safe plus she has made claims that a demon stalks her at night, could be a clue in his eyes.

The third and final file in his possession was that of a man named John Wallace. No criminal record on file, no signs of any violence in his past, pretty much a man on the straight and narrow. Which leads to the question, if the man is that squeaky clean, then why have the cops been keeping an eye on him?

"These can't be all the suspects." Grant fumed, tossing the files to the side. "Maybe the evidence will reveal more clues and lead me to a more solid suspect than these three." He reached for the file that contained pictures of the crime scenes, and of evidence collected by the forensics team. Looking through the pictures of the victims first, something caught his attention. Red marks around all six of their necks, by the angle he could tell the assailant attacked them from behind.

Next thing that caught his eye was the fact of certain body parts missing. Why would the killer take an eye, an ear, fingers, and toes from his victims? Could be that he thinks this is his way of revenge or justice. The killer washes away what he believes to be their sins with how he dresses the bodies up in certain clothing. Or leaving the victims out in the rain.

Grant set the pictures to the side and started going over what was collected. Pictures of rose petals are what Grant looked over first. This was a significant clue to maybe finding out the identity of the killer. Truth be told, this was a type of Japanese Rose, thus in the United States isn't easy to find. They only grow in the harshest of winters. Which would mean the killer is having them imported into one of the flower shops in town. The first thing to do will be to visit the flower shops in town, he thought to himself.

Next bit of evidence was the clothing he would dress the dead, some would be dressed in things that no average man could afford, while others were dressed poorly or not at all. This must have something to do with how he felt about each victim he would choose.

Then he noticed the position of how he left the bodies if Grant was right about the pictures they depicted that of good and evil. That would mean the murderer is fighting his own battle with what he believes is right and wrong, "Well that's enough looking through these files, nothing else I can learn without doing some investigating of my own." Grant placed the folders back in the suitcase and slid it under his bed. He then reached for his gun and holster, strapping it around his upper body. Once done he draped his coat over his shoulders, took a swig of bourbon and walked out of the hotel.

As Grant was walking towards his vehicle, the phone in his pocket started to ring. The number was from the Mayor's office, "Hello?" He clearly didn't want to answer, but the Mayor was his client like it or not."

"Did you get the package?"

"Yes sir," he said.

"And?"

"And what?"

"Any leads?"

"A few," Grant answered.

"Are you going to check into them?"

"Doing that now sir."

"Good, expect another phone call soon. Next time though I need results."

"Of course sir." Grant hung up the phone, placing it back in his pocket.

3

LOOKING INTO CLUES

There were only three flower shops in the town of Dover, and two of them Grant had no luck in finding the information he sought. He pulled up to the third and final shop hoping to find answers. Instead he found three men standing out front that he knew. It was Jason, Jimmy, and John. Three brothers that he had put away for dealing drugs before transferring to, New York.

This should be interesting, but Grant was determined to walk in and out of that flower shop regardless of the outcome. He opened the car door and cautiously got out of the vehicle. As he made his way towards the entrance, Jason blocked his way while Jimmy and John made sure that he couldn't turn back the way he came.

"Well if it isn't Mr. Dawson himself." Jason smirked, "How long has been since we seen him, last brothers?"

"Ten years to the day he put us in prison." John snarled.

"We've been waiting a long time to get our hands on you." Jimmy was punching the palm of his other hand. If Grant was right the man had the look of death in his eyes.

"Seeing how you're no longer a cop I say that is a plus for us," Jason said.

Grant smiled back at Jason, "I may not be a cop, but I am a private investigator. Which does give me the right to defend myself in any way I so chose."

Jimmy pushed Grant from behind then Jason punched him flush on the cheek which caused him to stagger a bit. "That felt damn good!" Jason howled. "Now come on, make this fun!" He punched him in the stomach causing him to bend over in pain. "Fight back!" Grant coughed up some blood and spate it on Jason's shoe. "You just made a big mistake." He went to punch Grant again, but he sidestepped Jason and shoved him into his brothers.

"Those two punches were on me," Grant said, wiping the blood from his mouth. "Now run along like good little boys before you get yourselves hurt."

"The only one that's going to get hurt is you," Jason said and went to throw another punch. Grant dodged the attack, kicking the side of Jason's knee. The man staggered and he took that as a chance to knock him out cold.

"You son of a bitch!" John shouted, charging after Grant.

Grant stepped to the side tripping John sending him crashing to the ground. Before he could get back to his feet, he was kicked in the face, knocking him out as well, like Jason before him. Jimmy stood there in silence watching and pondering the best course of action.

"Are you going to join in on the fun?" Grant asked.

The youngest of the brothers didn't answer, instead he turned tail and ran off down the sidewalk until he was out of sight. Grant shook his head with a smirk on his face. It was no surprise to him that Jimmy bailed on his brothers. He fixed his coat, straightened his hair and walked on inside the flower shop.

"Welcome to Abby's floral and home designs. How can I help you?"A young lady behind the counter smiled brightly.

He walked up to the counter and gave her a slight nod, "I believe that you can help me. My name is Grant Dawson, I'm a private investigator. I just need to ask you a few questions if that's alright."

"Of course," she replied. "By the way, my name is Tammy."

"Okay, Tammy. Does this place specialize in imported goods?"

"Like?" Tammy said.

"Japanese Roses, to be more specific," Grant said.

"Actually we do have those imported in for our most important customers."

"How many customers?"

"Four."

"Can I have their names?" Grant asked.

"Sorry, we don't know their names, and they usually send someone in to pick the flowers up for them."

"Is there one that orders in more than others?" He was going to keep asking questions until she gave him the answers he wanted. If that didn't work, he would have to go about things a different way.

"As a matter of fact, there is," Tammy replied.

Now we're getting somewhere, Grant thought to himself. "Is it a male or female that picks the flowers up?

"Male."

"Can you describe him to me?" This man sure was persistent, or at least that's how she felt.

Tammy had to think hard for a moment, "He was medium height, very thin, had quite a few tattoos."

"Anything about the man that stood out?" Grant was being pushy and the lady behind the counter just wanted him out of the store.

"The man wore an expensive earring in his right ear." She huffed giving him that look if he didn't leave she would call the cops.

He knew the young lady had enough of him, but at least he knew who she was referring to. It was a clear description of Leonard Clifton, the first suspect. "Thank you, ma'am." Grant nodded and smiled. "You have been very helpful." He turned and walked out of the flower-shop.

Outside he noticed that Jason and John had regained consciousness and ran off before the cops could be called, no surprise there. It was time for Grant to pay Leonard Clifton a little visit. As he was driving down the road. An all too familiar feeling started to build in the pit of his stomach. He was a professional and held his feelings at bay, putting his car in park Grant made his way inside the mechanic's shop where Leonard had been known to work.

"Can I help you?" A man covered in oil and grease asked.

"As a matter of fact you can," Grant replied. "I'm looking for, Leonard Clifton. Have you seen him?"

"Nope," the man answered. "Haven't seen him in weeks."

"Does he still work here?"

"Not anymore. His ass was fired. I gave that piece of shit plenty of chances and this is how he repays me? The man was I fool, I really thought he was turning his life around."

"Seems to me like you have a lot of hatred towards the man," Grant said.

"I'm his brother," the man replied. "I have every right to be mad."

"There's a difference between being mad, and having the blind hatred that I see in your eyes." Grant didn't want to reveal that he was a private investigator seeking information, instead he played on the man's emotions to get the answers he sought. "Why such anger towards family?"

"He used me, said he wanted to turn his life around, clean up his act and all that. I truly believed him this time around and gave him a job here, even got him a place to stay. Everything was going well until he started getting these weird phone calls. After that he was showing up late for work more and more until one day he just stopped coming in altogether."

"Did you answer the phone for your brother at all?" Grant's brow raised.

"I might have. Why?

"Could you tell me if the person calling was a male or female?"

"Not sure, the person was using one of those voice changing devices," the man answered.

"Damn," Grant muttered.

"Excuse me?"

"Can you give me your brother's address?" He quickly asked.

"Why are you so curious about my brother?" The look on his face was that of curiosity, nothing more.

"I just need a quick word with him is all," Grant insisted.

"Is he in trouble again?" The man huffed. "You know what, I don't care anymore." He wrote something down on a piece of paper and slid it across the counter. "You will find him here, I'm done talking." The man turned and walked away sticking true to his word.

The the address of where Clifton had been living over the past month or so. Was only a street down from where the last victim was found, bringing back that eerie feeling Grant was having earlier. Later that day he found himself standing outside of an old run-down apartment building. He glanced over the piece of paper again, apartment number thirty-eight was what it read. Doubt that I will find Mr. Clifton here, maybe if I'm lucky I will find a clue as to who he had been helping, Grant thought to himself.

The inside of the building was just as run down as the outside. There were holes in the walls, the carpet down the hallway was stained and chewed up by rats and small dogs. Plus the place smelled like urine, likely from animals and humans. As Grant made his way up the steps to the second floor, he had a gut feeling that he was being watched. In a place like this everyone is on edge, afraid of cops and drug dealers alike.

"Did Leonards brother know he was living such a place?" Grant muttered. "After all, he did say he helped him get a place to stay." He walked on until he came to a door with the number thirty-eight on the outside. Well here we are, maybe I should at least knock first. Doubt anyone is home though. He knocked on the door, no answer. He waited a minute or so and knocked again, still no answer.

“Nobody’s home, Mister," a voice said.

Grant turned to see a little girl in a dirty dress with matted blonde hair standing there looking up at him. "And what is your name little miss?" He knelt down and asked.

The little girl stood there swaying back and forth, with a big smile on her face. "Misty," she answered.

He returned the smile, "Such a cute name." Grant felt sorry for this little girl. Especially being forced to live in a dump like this, so he was going to be as friendly as possible.

"Thank you," she sheepishly smiled.

“Misty, can you tell me why you think Mister Clifton isn't home?"

"Mister Clifton, whistles when he walks down the hallway." She smiled brightly, "When he sees me, he likes to say hi and play games with me, he even tells me stories."

That doesn't sound like something Leonard would do, Grant thought to himself. He pulled out the picture of Leonard and showed it to Misty, "Is this the man that lives here? Is this, Mister Clifton?"

Misty shook her head, "No, I don't know that man. He looks like a bad person, I wouldn't talk to a scary man like that."

"I thought as much," Grant whispered. He looked back up at Misty with a smile on his face, "You've been a big help to me, Misty. I thank you for your help. Now run along, I have to confront the scary man in the picture." Misty's eyes got big, she turned and took off down the hallway.

He stood up, took a look around to make sure that no one was watching what he was about to do. He took a deep breath, readied himself and kicked the apartment door in. He walked on inside calmly like nothing had happened, shutting the door behind him. Grant walked around the apartment looking for any clues. So far the only thing he had found was pizza boxes with half eaten moldy food inside, and empty beer bottles scattered across the countertops along with a white substance.

By the looks of things no one has lived here for weeks, Grant thought to himself. Upon further investigation, he noticed how clean the kitchen sink and tub in the bathroom were. Odd that everything is dirty except the sink and tub. Then something else caught his attention, two small blood stains on the bathroom door. "Hmm, I have a bad feeling about this is. I believe the body that was found is that of Leonard Clifton himself." Grant looked around a little longer but there was nothing more to see.

It was a two-day drive but Grant had finally made it to the asylum that held Grace Jones, which is why he found it odd that she was on the list of suspects. Though before he could investigate Grant had to make a quick call to, Lieutenant Harris.

"Harris here, how can I help you?" His voice seemed a little edgy.

"Harris, it's me, Grant."

"Grant, where in the hell are you?!" Harris shouted. "I haven't heard from you in days."

"I've been doing some investigating of my own." His voice was shaky considering where he found himself, brought back some bad memories.

"Did you find anything worthwhile?"

"I found out the identity of our, John Doe," Grant replied.

"Who is it?" Harris sounded nervous now, not as angry as he was at first.

Grant lit up a cigarette taking a drag, smoke blew from his mouth as he said the words, "Leonard Clifton."

Harris went quiet for a brief moment, "Are you sure?"

"My investigation revealed clues that Leonard Clifton was unknowingly aiding the murderer. Or perhaps he knew all along, who knows for sure. Why Leonard was killed is still a mystery to me. If you compare the earring worn by the victim, you will see that it will lead you back to, Leonard Clifton."

"Damn," Harris grumbled. "Another lead ran cold. Oh well, does he have any family in the area?"

"Just his brother," Grant sighed. "But I don't think he really gives a damn if his brother is dead or alive." Sad to think that Clifton had no family that really gave a damn.

"Men like him burn bridges, they get all the second chances in the world while others get none. In the end, people like that get what they deserve." Harris's words were cold but true to a point.

"That was harsh, even for you."

"Pay no mind to me." Harris laughed, "Anyways, I need you to come into the station. Are you free?"

Grant let a cloud of smoke flow from his mouth, "Not at the moment, I'm paying a visit to, Grace Jones."

"Why?" Harris questioned.

"She may hold the key to solving this case."

"How so?"

"You will just have to trust me," Grant replied.

“Leave that poor woman alone,” Harris demanded. “She’s been through enough. Just come back to the station.”

“I can’t do that.” He didn't give Harris the chance to ask any more questions, as he hung up the phone.

A minute or so later Grant found himself standing outside the doors of the asylum. This wasn't something he was looking forward to, these places have always gave him the creeps. Talking to Grace Jones was of the utmost importance, yet still he found himself hesitating to walk inside. In the end, Grant beat back those anxious feelings forcing himself to walk through those doors.

Grant was quickly greeted by the staff on the other side, "Can I help you?" A tall, thin, pale looking man asked.

"Where I can find, Grace Jones?" Grant asked.

"Do you have the credentials you need to see her?" The man studied Grant closely, almost as if he was digging deep into his soul.

"I do." Grant pulled out some papers and handed them over to the man, "As you can see they are all signed and sealed by the mayor himself. So do yourself a favor and just lead me to her room."

The man looked over the papers ignoring the words of advice, "Everything seems in order."

Grant yanked the papers from the man’s hands, "Like I said before, lead me to her room," he demanded.

"Right this way." The man sighed turned and motioned for him to follow. Leading Grant down towards the end of a narrow hallway then stopped and pointed, "The last door to the right, I'm sure you can find your way from here." He turned and walked away, mumbling words of disgust under his breath.

Grant walked until he had gotten to the end of the hallway, standing outside of Grace Jones’s door. There was a small window that allowed him to peer inside. Grace was sitting on the edge of the bed rocking back and forth. Grant could tell this visit wasn't going to be as easy as his last when he met Bobby in a place exactly like this one. He opened the door slowly and let himself inside, "Grace? Grace Jones?" Grant hesitantly approached her, "Are you, Grace Jones?"

The lady stopped to look up at him, "Who wants to know?"

"My name is Grant Dawson, I'm a private investigator," Grant said. "I just need to ask you a few questions."

She had a faraway look in her eyes when she answered back, "Let me ask my friend, she makes all the decisions these days." Grace turned and started mumbling incoherent words, nodding along like someone was talking back to her. "Okay, Mr. Dawson. My friend gave me the go-ahead to talk with you."

Grant understood how to talk with someone that wasn't in the right frame of mind, though something seemed different about this one, "Thank you for allowing me to talk with, Grace." He was talking to nothing more than thin air, though it did make Grace happy. "Now, Grace. Did you know that you're on the suspect list for being a possible killer?"

"I had no idea," Grace said with a slight smile. "It doesn't surprise me though, with what happened and all."

"Why don't you tell me about that incident?"

"I bet you didn't know this, but I was once attacked by the murderer." Grace frowned with sadness but that quickly faded.

"It doesn't mention that in your files," Grant responded.

"The cop that worked my case didn't believe me." Grace sighed, "Not that I blame him, I was heavily addicted to drugs at one time. But I turned my life around after I almost died from an overdose. God gave me a second chance, and that madman tried to take it away from me. I fought him tooth and nail escaping his wrath with my life intact."

"If that was the case, how did you end up here?" He was wondering what in the hell was going on. If she was attacked by the killer why in the hell was she placed here?

"I was placed her because of my frail state of mind," Grace said.

“That doesn't make any sense.”

“Life doesn't make sense.” She shrugged.

"Tell me Grace, do you remember the name of the officer that worked that night?" Grant questioned.

"No, the drugs they give me here try my memory. I can barely remember anything at all these days."

He wasn't sure he trusted in her words, but he had other clues to look into. For now he had to leave her be, "Well Grace, sorry to keep you for so long. Thank you for being patient with me, and thank your friend for me as well. Have a good day, Grace." Grant turned to leave but she had one last thing to say.

"The man was right, I never did deserve a second chance in life. All roads would have led to this place in the end. At least I am making it up to him for God's mistake."

He wanted to tell her that whatever was said was nothing more than a lie. He wanted badly to turn around and tell her of all the great things she could accomplish outside these walls that held her prisoner. In the end, he walked out of the room without saying a word.

Back in his hometown of Dover, Grant's first course of action was to go visit Lieutenant Harris at the precinct. He pulled up to the police station, put the car in park and made his way inside. "Mr. Dawson." The receptionist smiled. "Lieutenant Harris has been expecting you."

"Well hello to you too, Mary." He smirked, "Been a while."

"Like I said Lieutenant Harris is expecting you." Mary grumbled.

Grant leaned on the counter with a smile on his face, "Don't you at least want to say hi?"

Mary was a beautiful young woman with red hair and pale skin, and just a few freckles on her forehead. Not only was Grant mesmerized by her pure beauty, she was also his ex-girlfriend. All of his memories of her were good ones, never once did he think poorly of her.

It was his fault in the first place that they had broken up. She wanted to go to college and he wanted to head for New York to join the N.Y.P.D. His desire to further his career and gain leverage into looking into his brothers' case was the only thing he cared for in life. Mary was tired of playing second place and wanted to focus on her own life for once. In the end both agreed to a mutual break up, it was for the best.

"Let's keep things professional, Mr. Dawson." Mary insisted. "Would you like for me to point you towards the Lieutenants office?"

He shook his head, "No thank you, Mary. I know my way around here still yet." He walked from one end of the building to the other, making sure to take a look into each room as he did so. It made him smile with pride knowing he was back at his old stomping grounds. This was the only place that made him feel like home.

"Grant!" An all to familiar voice called out. He turned around to see Harris with his head sticking out of his office door, "Get over here, we need to talk."

He walked over to greet Lieutenant Harris, "Sorry, I was taking a stroll down memory lane."

"You don't have to explain yourself to me," Harris said. "Have a seat, make yourself comfortable."

Grant took off his coat placing it on the coat rack. Afterwards walking over taking a seat at the Lieutenant's desk. That's when he noticed the papers there waiting for him, "What are these?"

"A minor inconvenience that needs to be taken care of." Harris smiled. Grant flipped through the pages, which seemed to draw the ire of his friend, "It's a police report from a few nights ago, all I need is for you to sign off. Don't you trust me?"

"A man can never be too careful." Grant reached for a pen and signed the papers as asked of him. "There." He pushed the papers back to the Lieutenant.

"That should keep the Captain off my back for a while." Harris joked. "Mary!"

Minutes later Mary came walking into the room, "What can I do for you, sir?" She glanced over at Grant but only for a moment.

"Run this to the Captain's office for me please." Harris handed the police report over to Mary.

"Right away sir." With the papers in hand she gave a faint smile and turned to leave the room.

He watched as Grant never took his eyes off Mary the whole time, "Does she bring back memories of old as well?" He asked.

Grant looked back at him with a half-hearted smile, "The sight of her brings back all kinds of thoughts. But the past is the past and that's something I don't like to discuss."

"You never were one for talking."

"Can we get down to business here, I do have other obligations." He shifted in his chair anxiously.

"Of course, of course." Harris laughed.

Grant ignored the laughter and with a serious look he asked, "Was I right about our victim?"

The laughing stopped, the time for jokes were over these were matters that did not need to be taken lightly. "Leonard Clifton was the John Doe we found at the crime scene."

"Did you phone his brother?"

"Yep."

"And?"

"He didn't seem to care." Harris shrugged, not once showing any kind of sympathy.

"Unfortunate." Grant sighed.

"Can't say I blame him," he nonchalantly replied. "Anyways, did you find anything of use in your talk with, Grace?"

Just like over the phone Grant could hear the tone of Lieutenant Harris's voice change when they talked about, Leonard Clifton. He was sure it was the man's way of tuning out all of the bad he had experienced over the years as a cop, so he didn't think any more of it. Still yet, he didn't feel like he could trust the man completely. "I couldn't make heads or tails of what she was trying to tell me."

"I did say it would be a waste of time," he replied, clasping his hands tightly together. "Have you found out anything else?"

Refusing to tell him about his visit to the flower-shop, or the fact that he went to Leonard's apartment building. Though Grant had a feeling that he already knew, "I do hope to find out more throughout the week."

Harris wasn't done asking questions, but his time was cut short when Mary re-entered the room, "Sorry to bother you, Lieutenant." Mary nervously smiled.

"What do you need, Mary?" Harris asked.

"Captain Simons needs to have a word with you," Mary answered.

"Let her know that I will be right there."

"Will do sir." Mary nodded before walking out of the room.

Harris stood up from his chair, "We both know I can't keep the Captain waiting." He extended his hand.

Grant took hold of his hand with a firm grip, "True, we both know that she's a maneater." Both men laughed.

"Take care out there." He released his grip on Grant's hand, "One last thing."

"What is it?"

"Don't dig too deep into this case, you might not like what you find." It seemed more like a warning than anything else. He slapped him on the shoulder and walked out the door.

Grant was left to his own devices, he had two options to choose from, leave or search his old friend's office. It wasn't something that he wanted to do personally, but looking through Harris's office could prove fruitful. If luck would have it, he might be able to find the complete file on, Grace Jones. Which in turn will lead him to the officer that placed her in the asylum in the first place.

His search proved pointless. The only files he found was that of old cases that Lieutenant Harris had solved and the medals he received for doing so. The office didn't reveal much about his old friend or the case either. But a picture on the top of the desk caught Grant's attention.

It was a photo of Harris with his wife, and standing in the middle was a teenage girl in a graduation gown and cap holding onto a Japanese Rose. I didn't know that Harris had a kid, Grant thought to himself. Maybe I will ask him about it later.

"Mary, it was nice seeing you again." Grant threw his coat over his shoulder. She didn't even bother to give him a second glance, "I deserve the cold shoulder. It took all I had to walk away from this town, from everything that I had ever known, even from you. Know that you were always on my mind, I just hope that one day you will understand why maybe even forgive me."

He went to walk out of the precinct when Mary called out to him, "Wait!" He paused momentarily to glance back at her, "Would you." She took a deep breath. "Would you like to have lunch with me sometime?” It took all she had to ask that question. But she needed some closure before she could move on with her life completely.

“Of course.” He grinned from ear to ear. "When?"

"Not tonight." She sighed, "How about, Friday?"

"Sounds good, Mary." Grant walked away whistling.

It was late at night when he pulled his vehicle into the hotel parking. As he was getting ready to exit the vehicle his phone began to ring. He glanced at the screen and it said "private" number. Grant was hesitant to answer at first, then he remembered that most of his clients called him in a manner such as that, "Grant's private investigation services, how can I help you?”

"Hello, Mr. Dawson." The voice sounded distorted. It was clear this person was using a device to hide his or her real voice.

"Who is this?"

"Somebody you've been tracking." The voice proclaimed.

"The professed, Midnight Killer." Grant huffed, “So we finally get a chance to talk.”

Whoever was on the other line found his remark funny, "That is the name the media has given me, yes. Though that name means nothing to me this is not something I do for the attention."

"Coming from one that kills others and hangs them up for the world to see does not want attention," he responded. "I find that hard to believe."

"Believe what you will," the man said. "It matters not to me. In your mind you think of me as nothing more than a killer, a madman that murders just to feed his own ego. A man that is battling his demons, trying to figure out which side of himself is good or evil. Am I right?"

That was my words to a tee earlier, how would he know that? "Is that not true?"

"It's the furthest thing from it." Laughter ensued on the other end of the phone. "There are those who deserve a second chance in life and those who don't. Simple is it not?”

"And you decide who deserves that second chance in life." Grant boiled over with anger.

"Tell me something Mr. Dawson, does it not aggravate you that drug dealers, rapist and child molesters get a second chance while others do not?"

Grant had to admit that deep down inside he felt the same way, but that doesn't give anyone the right to take the law into their own hands, "It doesn't give you the right to murder them."

"Someone has to do something!"

"Even if you kill an innocent, like Jake White!"

"You really believe that he was innocent?" The person on the other end chuckled.

"He was a straight-A student, on his way to a great college and you snuffed out his life before it even got started." Grant argued. "Explain that to me you piece of shit!"

"Jake White was not innocent!" The person's voice raised. "His drunk driving killed an eighteen-year-old child that had her whole life ahead of her. But who got the second chance? Jake, the drunk little rich boy that had mommy and daddy there to get his sorry ass out of trouble. Did he pay for his crimes? No, he never spent one damn day behind bars. Tell me, is that justice?"

“Even if that's the case it doesn't give you the freedom to judge others, to punish them the way you see fit.”

"This conversation has run its course, Mr. Dawson. It was never intended to go this far. I only called to give you a warning, stop digging, stop trying to find out my identity. Leave this town and all that remains behind you or the people you care for will pay the price in your place."

"Your threats mean nothing to me!" Grant snapped.

"Is that so?" The other laughed at his boldness, "If that's the case, then I'm sure you wouldn't mind if I paid that pretty little redhead a visit down at the police station."

"You stay away from her!" Grant slammed his hand down on the steering wheel, "If you even get near her I will find you and kill you myself!"

"Seems that I have struck a nerve," the voice responded. "Does that mean we are on the same page now?"

"Let me explain something to you," he said with hatred in his voice. "One way or another I will find you and I will stop you. And I won't stop until I do that much I can promise."

"That's a shame, Mr. Dawson. Remember that I tried to warn you, the blood that will be shed next is in your hands." With a click, the person on the other side ended the call.

Dawson glanced back at the screen on his phone, somehow any sign of a call had disappeared. Whoever this person was, knows how to tap phones, delete information and keep tabs on others. They've had experience in surveillance that much was certain which made his belief of this possibly being the work of a cop that much stronger.

4

A GAME OF CAT AND MOUSE

THAT NIGHT WHEN GRANT HAD RETURNED TO HIS HOTEL ROOM A LARGE sized yellow envelope lay in the center of the floor, waiting for his eyes only. He reached down to pick it up, atop it read in big red letters "Mr. Dawson." Deep down he knew who the package was from, the question was did he want to play the madman's game. At that point he didn't have a choice, he was already in to deep and refused to give up now. If he didn't put an end to the murderer now, someone he cared for could be hurt or even killed.

The man cringed at the thought of what could be inside the envelope. His fingers cautiously ran down each side of the yellow paper, trying to detect what might be within. He ripped the end of the envelope right off, shaking the contents out onto his bed. At first glance, there seemed to be pictures and a small cassette tape along with a hand-held tape player that lay atop the bed.

"The murderer worked fast to put this together in just a few hours since we last spoke," Grant muttered. "Or maybe he already knew I would refuse to leave and planned this ahead of time." He reached down and picked up the tape and cassette player, placing the tape in the cassette and pressed play.

"Hello, Mr. Dawson." It was the same distorted voice from before,

"Remember me? I'm sure you do, I'm the person you've been chasing for the past few days. You see, I knew you wouldn't leave town, nor walk away from this case, I think you figured that out as well. Let's not get into that right now. We need to discuss something more important, if I'm right, you're probably wondering what that is."

The next thing Grant heard sent chills throughout his body. There was another voice on the tape but very faint, he could barely make out the sounds of someone begging for their life. Shortly after the killer demanded his hostage to shut the fuck up.

"Damn it." As much as he wanted to do something to help, he could not. The situation was out of his hands, for now all he could do at this point was pay close attention to the rest of the recording.

"Can you hear this girl begging for her life? I could kill her right now, but don't worry I'm not going to do that, you are. You see Dawson, the choices you make will decide this young ladies fate. I am going to bury her alive with just enough oxygen to last forty-eight hours. If she truly deserves a second chance, you will be the one to save her life.

Since we have the truth of the matter out of the way. Allow me to explain to you how this game is going to work. There are several pictures you need to look through with little-hidden clues on this girls whereabouts. I would have left you a map as well, but you already know this town like the back of your hand. Question is, will you make the right choice? Remember, this girl's life is in your hands."

With that the recording ended, he had to go to work quickly and decisively. His first plan of action was to call Lieutenant Harris and have him meet at the police station. Then grab everything that was in the envelope and rush over to the precinct.

Harris was there to greet Grant at front of the station, "What's going on, Grant? You sounded upset over the phone."

"No time to explain, just follow me." Grant rushed past the Lieutenant and on inside the precinct. Marching straight through the lobby and into the meeting room.

Turner was in the room talking with a fellow officer when private investigator barreled through the door startling him, "What in the hell is the meaning of this?" He hissed.

"I don't have time for your mouth right now, Turner!" Grant fired back.

The officer looked over his superior, "Can you not keep control over your friend?"

"The man does as he pleases." Harris shrugged.

"Not here he doesn't." Turner reached into his pocket and pulled out a pair of handcuffs, "I'm placing you under arrest."

Harris stepped in between Grant and Officer Turner, "Not on this night, Turner. Leave him be." Harris told him.

"Step aside, Lieutenant." Turner warned.

"Don't forget that I'm still your commanding officer!" He took a deep breath to calm his nerves, "Do us both a favor and stand down." Harris retorted.

"I'm sure the Captain will want to hear of this." Turner was clearly threatening his superior.

"Then go and get her." Grant interrupted. "The Captain will surely want to hear what I have to say."

The young cop was mad as hell that Lieutenant Harris had let this man take control of the precinct. Even though he wanted to throw Dawson in jail, Turner couldn't do so without a good reason or permission from his superiors. He backed up, putting the handcuffs away mumbling a few words under his breath before storming out of the room.

The Lieutenant acted as though nothing had transpired and began questioning his friends reason for his brashness, "Are you going to explain yourself now? For your sake, this had better be good or the Captain will have your ass in a vise."

Grant handed Harris the tape player, "Listen to this."

"What is this?"

"Save the questions for later. First listen, then we talk."

He pressed play, listening to every word that was said on the tape. Grant watched the Lieutenant's facial expression, expecting to see some kind of emotion. The man showed no sign of even caring one way or the other. His face remained stone cold as he glanced back up, "Anything else?"

"Is that all you have to say?" Grant was taken aback by how the Lieutenant reacted.

"Well I need to know." Harris shrugged.

Glaring at his old friend, something about Harris didn't sit well with him. The Lieutenant had been acting strange lately, either it had to do with his return or the fact he was there to look into the midnight killer case. Maybe the man felt like he was stepping on his toes, looking into a case that he had been working on for years, "Just these pictures he mentioned." Offering Harris the photos.

Reaching out to take the pictures, he began to thumb through them one at a time. It was then that Captain Simon's and Officer Turner barged into the room. "Why is this man in my precinct? And why did you stop Turner from making a rightful arrest?" Simon's angrily asked.

Tossing the tape player over to Simon's, "Here, that has all the answers you need," Harris responded.

After listening to the tape, she was in a state of disbelief. It was hard to say if fear or anger flooded over her face, possibly a little of both. "Where are the pictures the madman went on about?"

"The Lieutenant has them," Grant said.

"Do you think this man is playing a game? Or do you believe in what this recording says?" Simon's questioned.

"I believe what I hear," Harris said. "This person is unhinged, their mindset is different than ours. If Grant doesn't feed into what this maniac wants an innocent person will die."

"Why did the killer choose Dawson instead of one of us?" Turner grumbled. "Unless he's in on it in some way."

Grant grabbed Turner by the collar of his shirt and slammed him against the wall with force. "Listen to me you stupid son of a bitch! I'm not in league with the killer, and if you accuse me of that again I will make you pay." He wanted to snap Turner like a twig and the urge to do so was strong.

"Mr. Dawson!" The Captain shouted. "Let Officer Turner go this instant. Or I will personally see you behind bars!"

Harris walked up to Grant and put his hand on his shoulder, "Let him go, Turner is not worth it and you know it. How can you help anyone if you're in jail?" He released his grip on the officers shirt giving him one last shove against the wall again for good measure. "Good. Now let's get this mess figured out."

"Not so fast!" Turner hissed. "You put your hands on an officer of the law, Dawson. I hereby place your ass under arrest, let's see how you like being behind bars for once."

"Knock it off, Turner!" Harris demanded.

"How about you step out of my way!" The young man fired back.

"Shut the hell up and act like you want to help save this girl's life!" Simon's shouted.

"Sorry, Captain." Turner coughed, "I lost sight of what was important there for a second. It won't happen again."

"See that it doesn't!" She focused her gaze solely on the Lieutenant, "And what about you?"

"What about me?" Harris asked.

"Do you have anything you would like to say?" Simon's said.

"Nope." He shrugged.

Grant was watching the three of them bicker amongst themselves, he felt like this was his doing and needed to stop the bleeding. "Sorry to interrupt, but if you want to save that girl like you say, Captain. Then we all have to cool our tempers, put our egos to the side and work together. If we don't, she is as good as dead."

"He's right," the Lieutenant said. "Wouldn't you agree, Turner?" The officer stared daggers at Harris but never said a word, just nodded instead. The Lieutenant grinned slyly at the young officer, it was his way of letting him know that he was still in control. Harris held up the pictures, "If what the killer said on the recording is true, these photos hold the key to saving the life of his chosen victim. To be honest though I can't make heads or tails of these so-called clues."

"Let me take a look." The Captain reached for the photos, and Harris obliged. "Hmm." She thumbed through the pictures, but the look on her face proved that not even she could figure out the clues hidden within the photos.

"You look confused Captain," Grant said.

"I don't know exactly what to look for."

"Can I have a look?" Grant asked.

"Have you not looked them over already?" She questioned.

"Not yet," he replied. "I came here right away to meet with, Harris."

"Take them." She handed the photos over, "If you find anything, and I mean anything at all, you had better let me know.

"Will do." He nodded.

"As long as you are working this case, Mr. Dawson. You will have full access to this facility," Simon said. "Don't make me regret it." She then turned and left the men to their own devices. But what she didn't know was that Dawson had the aid of the Mayor and could enter anytime he pleased.

"What's our first move?" Turner asked. Not that he enjoyed the fact he had to work with Grant in the first place.

"You plan on helping?" Grant responded.

"As much as I can." Turner insisted. "Doesn't mean I trust you, nor do I like you for that matter."

"Then why help?"

"I want to help save that girls life."

"That's good enough for me." Grant cracked a faint smile. Even though he would rather kick the young man's ass, he needed all the help he could get.

"What would you have me do?" Turner asked.

"Go and retrieve the recording I brought in from Captain Simon's. Listen to it over and over again for any sounds of dripping water, or any kind of echoes. There might be something there that could lead us to where he keeps his victims captive. I will look over these pictures for clues, while Harris will get things ready to go for when we find out where the victim is buried."

The men went straight to work, Turner grabbed the tape recorder as asked of him. He listened to the recording for several hours straight without stopping once. Harris went out and found shovels, pickaxes, and anything else that could be used to dig up an unmarked grave. Grant stayed behind at the precinct and focused solely on looking over the pictures the murderer had sent to him. This was the hardest of jobs because the victim's life hung in the balance of the choices he would make.

The clock was ticking, it was a race against time and a whole twenty-four hours had passed. That meant the young lady that had been taken against her will only had another twenty-four hours to go before her oxygen would run out. The thought of that young lady's air running out and suffocating to death drove Grant to the brink of madness, yet he held his composure until he had put the pieces together.

"I found something!" He announced.

Turner was the only other person in the room at the time, listening to the recording for the second day. Grant's voice carried over to him and through his headphones and it made him jump, "Is something wrong? Or did you find something of importance?" He jumped up out of his chair wanting to know what Grant had learned.

"I did find something, if I'm right I know where the young lady is buried." He was happy to give out good information for once.

"Thank god, I have to let Captain Simon's and Lieutenant Harris know." He ran out of the room with haste. A minute later he had returned with his superiors. Lieutenant Harris, didn't seem like he cared for the news he had received. As for the Captain, she was ready to act at a moments notice.

"What did you find?" Simon's wanted quick responses and she wanted them right then and there.

"I need to show you rather than tell you," Grant responded. "That way you can understand how the murderer thinks, how he works and most of all how it relates to me."

"Okay Dawson, show us what you have found," she said.

"Let's get started." He walked over to one of the tables in the room and placed four different pictures on the top, "Take a look at these pictures, there is a reason the murderer sent them to me."

"Why is that?" Turner asked.

"Look at the first picture closely it's of the local diner, Mack's Down Home Cooking," Grant explained. "This is where Mary and myself, had our first date. And this picture is of Mary's home, where I kissed her for the first time." He paused for a second and pointed at the third picture, "See this one?"

"That's the towns bowling alley," Turner replied. "What does any of this have to do with finding that girl?"

"I'm getting to that. If you would look at the fourth and final photo. You will see a tree where initials are carved in the front."

"Yours and Mary's no doubt," Harris said, almost as if he knew ahead of time. But everyone in the room was caught up in finding the latest victim they paid no mind to how quickly he responded.

"Exactly." Grant nodded.

"What does this have to do with the missing girl?" Simon's interjected once more.

He reached for a sharpie and circled a spot on the picture, "This is where the missing girl is buried." He insisted.

"Are you sure?" Simon's asked.

"No offence Dawson but we can't go on a hunch." Turner added.

"There's no doubt in my mind you will find the girl there." Grant assured them.

"Then what are we waiting for, let's go save a life," Simon's said with excitement. Of course, she was happy, this would go a long way towards getting her re-elected as Captain for a third term.

"I'm afraid it won't be that simple." The look on Grant's face telling a grim tale.

"All we have to do is dig her up before the oxygen tank runs out," Turner said.

Harris walked up to Turner placing his hand on his shoulder. "Think about, does this lunatic ever leave his victims alive?"

He swatted Harris's hand off his shoulder, "Did you forget about Grace Jones? He let her live didn't he?"

"That was a mistake!" Harris snapped. "I doubt he will let that happen again. Grow up and face the facts, the girl is dead-"

"We don't know anything for sure." The Captain interrupted.

"Then let's find out," Harris replied with a cold tone to his voice. He reached for the mic that was clipped to his belt, holding it up close to his mouth he hit the button on the side. "This is Lieutenant Harris, I need all available officers to meet me at Grayson Park. I repeat I need all available officers to meet me at Grayson Park."

After the Lieutenant made the call for all available officers to meet at the park, it was only a matter of time before the area was filled with the men and women of law enforcement. If the young lady was still alive like they had hoped, then time wasn't on their side. Harris and Simon's lead the charge, they both had Grant take them to where he believed the girl was buried. When they had gotten to the tree with the initials. Harris made sure everyone had a shovel in their hands digging.

The group of officers shoveled dirt well into the evening when one person would begin to wear down, another would step in and take their place. When things seemed to be going well, like always, it started to rain, just a little at first. In this little town when it rains it pours, and that's exactly what it began to do. With the rain coming down, the hole they had dug was filling with water at an alarming rate. They had to work even faster or the girl could drown from the rainwater.

"Keep digging!" The Captain shouted. "There is no time to switch with the other group!" The rain was coming down hard, and the grave was filling fast. The situation looked grim, they were five feet into the ground and have yet to find any signs of a coffin. At this point if they didn't find something soon, they would have to call off the rescue or risk the chance of losing one of their own. "We have no choice but to call off the rescue!" Simon's demanded. But Grant refused to give up, while everyone else was climbing out of the grave, he stayed and kept digging. "Mr. Dawson, I gave you a direct order. Get out now!"

He shook his head, "I won't give up, not until I know for sure!"

"Is it worth dying for?" Harris hissed.

"It is if it will lead me to that sick freak!" Grant shouted back. He kept digging, throwing mud in all directions with the shovel, muttering to himself as he did so. It was clear that he was losing control, but not a single person dare tried to stop him. He lifted his shovel high above his head in defiance and slammed it into the mud. This time it wasn't just mud that the shovel had hit, he was sure he had finally found the wooden coffin. “Did you hear that?”

“Hear what?” Simon's replied.

“Listen!” He hit the ground with the end of the shovel twice more. There was a thud each time, “See, there is something here! Help me get it out of the ground!”

“You heard the man!” Simon's shouted. “Get down there and help, Mr. Dawson!”

Another five or six minutes of digging had gone by, with the added weight of carrying buckets of water out of the grave as well. With their efforts, the officers had managed to get the wooden coffin up out of the ground. Everyone was completely exhausted from all the hard work, but it was time to see if their efforts to save the young girl's life were in vain.

Grant didn't bother with knocking on the coffin or offering his voice for reassurance. He knew what he would find inside, there was no hint of urgency now that he had the wooden box out of the ground. But Officer Turner had a crowbar in hand desperately praying at the lid. “Don't just stand there, help me!”

Grant picked up a pry bar of his own and helped pry the lid loose. He stood on one side and Turner on the other, they both lifted the top right off and tossed it to the ground. The young officer was the first to look inside, hoping and praying that he helped save a life on this day. When Turner turned away vomiting, Grant got the answer he was looking for.

It was then that Grant looked inside the coffin, it was as he had thought, the girl was already dead. The poor woman had been killed in the most hanice of ways, she had been tortured due to the deep cuts on her arms and legs. Both her index fingers were cut from her hands, and it looked like her earrings were pulled from her ears with a lot of force. The young lady had been through hell and back, only to be suffocated by the killer in the end.

"You were right, Mr. Dawson." Simon sighed,"This was nothing more than a game of cat and mouse. He wanted us to find her this way."

"Correction, he wanted me to find her here as a clear warning to me."

"Why would the killer do that?" Simon's asked.

"Don't worry about that right now." Grant cleared his throat, "Let's take a closer look at the body."

"All I see is how the maniac tortured and killed another victim," Turner said.

"Look past that." Grant insisted.

"What are we looking for?" The Captain questioned.

"More clues."

Lieutenant Harris broke his silence with a question of his own, "Is there a need to do this in the rain? It's cold as hell out here, clearly the girl is already fucking dead."

The comments made by his old friend caught Grant by surprise, "Odd that you of all people would say something like that." He studied him for a moment longer, "You know that if you move the body around too much in the rain crucial evidence could be lost."

"Then point out what we are looking for so we can get the hell out of here." The man grumbled.

Grant took a mental note of how frequently Lieutenant Harris's state of mind would drastically change from time to time, this day was no different. Again this wasn't the time to ponder on such things. "Take a very close look at this young lady's throat." Grant pointed, "See how it's swollen. If you take a flashlight and look inside her mouth, you can clearly see that the killer pumped her throat full of silicon.Think about it for a second, if the killer can skin a person alive, kidnap a girl and fill her throat with silicon without being found out. Then he has to be doing so from a secluded area, or a large building."

"Like a warehouse of some kind," Turner said.

"Perhaps."

About that time the coroner walked up, asking if everyone would leave. He needed to collect evidence and get the body back to the lab. While the others were heading back to the warmth of their vehicles, and the coroner was busy gathering the evidence. Grant caught a glimpse of another large yellow envelope, with haste he reached down and picked up the package. He hid the envelope out of sight in his coat before walking away.

5

LOOKING THROUGH THE EYES OF A KILLER

THE TIME WAS AROUND ELEVEN O'CLOCK AND GRANT HAD CONSUMED half a bottle of whiskey. His mind was still on what the others and himself had found inside the coffin. Even though he didn't expect to find the young lady alive, it didn't make things any easier. He also had the yellow envelope sitting on the table in front of him. He debated on opening the package to check the contents inside.

Grant wasn't afraid of what he would find, he was upset with himself that the murderer was still at large, still killing. He thought for sure that with the tape player and the pictures in his possession, he would find some clue that would help identify the killer. A familiar noise on the recording, or perhaps a fingerprint, but it was not to be. The killer was smart and left no traces behind, except a promise of another kill if Grant didn't leave town.

That thought stuck in his head, what would the madman do next if he didn't find a way to stop him. Who would be his next victim? Mary? Or perhaps another person from the street that was deemed unworthy. That thought alone was enough to make Grant reach for the envelope. Ripping it open, letting the contents inside fall on top of the table.

A VHS tape, Grant thought to himself as he reached out for the item. He looked on the table for anything else but apparently, that was all to the package. He flipped the tape over where he found writing in the same red letters as before. "Play Me" is what it read. "I doubt this shithole will have a VCR I can use." Grant muttered. He smirked when he realized who he could go to if he wanted to view the tape. This time it would have to be in secret. He didn't want Captain Simon's or Officer Turner to find out about what he held in his hands. He pulled up to the precinct yet again, this time though he casually walked inside.

"Another late night visit yet again?" Mary snarked.

"What can I say, it's hard to stay away from such a beautiful woman."

"Flattery will get you nowhere with me, Dawson."

"Maybe you will see things differently on our date." Grant smirked.

"It's not a date." Mary grumbled. "If you're looking for Lieutenant Harris, he's not here." She changed the subject rather quickly.

"Not needing to talk with him this time." He didn't push the subject of them meeting up on Friday. If he still wanted that to happen he knew his best bet would be to back off. "Just need the use of the surveillance room is all."

"Does Captain Simon's have knowledge of this?"

"As long as I am working a certain case, I am allowed use of this facility," Grant answered. "Her words, not mine. You can even call the Mayor if you like." Even though Simon's meant the case of the kidnapped girl that was buried alive, not actually what he was doing at that moment. But what the hell, if he could bring a killer to justice then he would use any means necessary.

"You better not be lying to me." Mary warned.

"Trust me, just this once," Grant said. "This is important."

She could see the level of seriousness in his eyes, she knew how serious he could be. And when he has that look he doesn't give up. "Have it your way," she replied. "Make sure you don't get me fired." Mary pushed the button under the counter to unlock the door, "Don't touch anything back there either, remember I'm not supposed to let anyone back there except for police officers."

"Thank you." Grant smiled.

"Don't mention it," Mary said. "Seriously, don't mention this to anybody."

Grant walked on ahead through the door, it shut and locked behind him. He casually made his way down the hall and to the left. He walked his way inside the surveillance room looking around until he found a TV connected to a VCR. He reached into his coat and removed the tape. Grant turned the TV on then placed the tape inside the VCR and hit the play button. He turned the volume up just enough so he alone could hear and nobody else.

The recording started off fuzzy with very little noise, then the picture slowly became clear. Grant looked on, his face filled with rage when he came to the realization of who was being recorded. It was the young lady the maniac had kidnapped and killed. She was sobbing and begging for her life. He recorded the last minutes of that poor girl's life, Grant thought to himself.

"Shut the hell up!" a voice shouted from off the screen.

"The killer likes to use the same voice distortion device in all of his recordings and phone calls." Grant muttered. "Wonder why?"

"Please let me go," the girl pleaded. "I won't tell anyone what you've done, I promise."

A figure walked into the view of the camcorder, whoever it was, was wearing a black Halloween costume. There was no mask just a black hood that had glowing red eyes emanating from underneath. "Please let me go, I won't tell anyone," the mysterious figure mocked. This person used their hand to brush the girl's hair out of her face, "Don't you worry your pretty little head, Amy. I will let you go after we have some fun."

"Why are you doing this to me?" She cried out.

"Because you're a mistake. God let you have a second chance in life when you didn't deserve it. Your crimes have gone unpunished for long enough." The figure retorted.

"I don't know what you're talking about!" Amy screamed.

"Then allow me to refresh your memory." The figure opened up what looked to be an old pocket knife. "What about the drugs? Do you remember prostituting your body out for money?" Each word that was said was followed by a slash of the knife. The blade sinking into Amy's flesh causing her to writhe in pain. "How about stealing from your dying grandmother just to support your addiction! Do you deny that?!"

"No." Amy whimpered, tears running down her cheeks.

"You have one chance to explain your actions and you better make it good. If not you die!" The killer laughed in her face mocking her emotions, enjoying every moment.

"I was in a bad place in my life." Amy cried, "I did wrong but I got help with my addiction, even found god."

"I see, so you got a second chance even though your own grandmother died with a broken heart after she witnessed you stealing from her. I ask you, is that fair?" The crazed figure turned to look at the camcorder, eyes still glowing red, "Tell me, Dawson. Does this sound like a person that deserves what was given to her? Hmm, whatever should I do? I would ask you Mr. Dawson, but you already know how this plays out."

"Let me go!" Amy begged.

"Well I did promise after we played I would set you free," the murderer said. The person walked out of view from the camera for a minute or so returning with a syringe.

"What are you going to do with that?" Amy nervously asked.

"Giving you your freedom." The black figure leaned in with the syringe sticking the needle into Amy's neck, injecting a foreign substance into her esophagus. The person then went over to the camcorder and removed it from the stand. This maniac thought it would be fun to give Grant a bird eyes view of what was about to happen. "Allow me to show you my masterpiece." The camcorder was held up to the young girls face, one minute she's crying and begging for her life. The next she's gasping for air where there was none.

She fought against the straps that had her bound, she even tried to scream but no words would come. Soon her body would succumb to the lack of oxygen. Amy's eyes turned blood red, her chest that frantically sought air would move no more, she had suffocated to death.

Grant looked away from the TV briefly, "Son of a bitch." He closed his eyes fighting the urge to knock over the TV. It was hard for him to keep watching the tape, but he had to finish what he had started. If he didn't find a way to stop this crazed psychopath, more lives would surely be taken.

When he glanced back at the recording, the camera was still on Amy's face, except this time the killer was caressing her face. "Such a beautiful young lady," the figure said. "Had the whole world in her hands and threw it all away. Became nothing more than a wasted life. Sad wouldn't you say, Mr. Dawson? But I do have one question for you. How does it feel to look through the eyes of a killer?" He or she laughed, and laughed, and laughed until the screen went fuzzy again and the tape ended.

Dawson took the tape from the VCR and got the hell out of there, he didn't even bother to stop and say goodbye to, Mary. She was caught off guard by how quickly he rushed by her and out of the precinct. Mary questioned what may have gotten to him. Though at that time it didn't matter, there was no use pondering on such trivial things.

Another hour would come and go as Mary waited for her replacement. Like all other times, she stayed behind for some small talk before calling it a night. She only lived a few blocks away from the precinct, so she never had to worry about driving or catching the bus. On this night walking home something seemed different. Mary had this strange feeling that she was being watched. Unsure if she was in danger or not, she picked up the pace.

Her heart raced as sounds of footsteps followed behind her. Mary was sure that whoever was behind her had bad intentions. She felt as though if she didn't get home soon she wouldn't make it. When she made it to her apartment the feeling of dread crept over her.

She fumbled around inside her purse trying to find the keys to the building. A sense of urgency was swirling in the pit of her stomach. She thought for sure if she didn't get inside the apartment complex fast enough, she would be swept away into the night. Mary grabbed the keys removing them from her purse with haste, she fumbled with each key one at a time.

Her heart was racing, Mary was beginning to worry that she would never get inside to where safety awaited. Lucky for her she had found the key to the lock and let herself inside. Mary quickly locked the door behind her, letting out a sigh of relief. She was in the safety of her home or so she thought. That night time went by as usual, Mary sat in her chair drinking a hot cup of tea and reading her book.

Afterward, she did her nightly routine, took her sleeping pills, did a few situps and pushups before taking a shower. The whole time she was unaware that someone had let themselves inside her apartment, watching her every move. The intruder slithered out from under the bed like a snake, while she was sleeping. If this was indeed the murderer they had changed into a different type of costume.

This person dressed in black but donned a white mask that had a big grin and crazy looking eyes. With a camera in hand, he or she snapped pictures of her apartment and of her sleeping. Before walking away the intruder leaned in close and watched Mary, caressed her cheek, and whispered, "I will see you again very soon."

Morning would come quicker than what Grant had expected. He stayed up all night looking over the clues from the crime scenes, plus everything the killer had sent him. In his mind he thought that he had missed something crucial. And he intended on figuring out what that might have been. If he was going to do so, then he needed to visit the very first crime scene that took place so many years ago.

Grant took another swig of whiskey before darting out the door of his hotel room. Now driving down the highway towards his destination, deep in thought about the case. That is until he noticed that his cell phone was beeping. He had a missed call, followed by a voicemail. Grant placed his Bluetooth in his ear and called his voicemail inbox. The voicemail was another warning from the killer himself, "Tick tock, tick tock. Time is running out, if you're not gone by tonight you shall surely pay."

He made up his mind long ago that he wasn't going to let some maniac run him out of town. This was a job he was going to see through to the end, no matter the cost. It was a choice that Grant had made when he first arrived on the scene, even before then. He knew the risk when he accepted the job from the Mayor, but that wasn't a factor in his decision to return.

His family's well being was of no concern to him, his dad died when he first joined the police force. Shortly after his mom took his younger brother and moved away. As far as friends went, he didn't have many, and they turned their backs on him when he joined the N.Y.P.D. All except for Harris, who had a chance to go to New York, but stayed behind to become a Lieutenant, and he can take care of himself.

The only person that meant anything to him was, Mary. He still had feelings for her, but if he wasn’t careful that would lead to his downfall. Solving this case before another innocent could get hurt was his top priority. Or perhaps something more was driving him on.

Grant drove his car down a dirt road, both sides filled with rows of corn as far as the eye could see. The land was owned by a farmer named, Bradley Wilson. When he was a kid him and his older brother John Boy would play hide and seek here. He didn't know much about Bradley Wilson, other than the fact that the man kept to himself and hated when others intruded on his land.

Fact remains that the first body was found on his property. When asked he claimed that someone must have stolen his tractor, torn up his cornfield and left the dead body there to frame him. Bradley was eventually taken off the list of suspects due to the lack of evidence tying him to the crime. Still everyone was a suspect, didn't matter if you were friend or foe.

Pulling up to where the first crime scene took place, he put the car in park and got out of the vehicle. He made his way through the corn stalks until he got to the area where the corn, for some reason refused to grow. It was an anomaly that occurred every so often. Mainly where a murder took place, or where a body was placed. Grant walked the area hoping to find clues that the police might have missed. The search didn't prove as fruitful as he had wished.

But what if this isn't one of those weird anomalies? What if the killer used a very potent weed killer that actually kept the corn from growing in this area. Though there were no dead corn stalks left behind it wouldn't matter. He didn't have the luxury of a forensic teams help on this case, nor did he want it either.

The man had another way to tell if the area had indeed been sprayed with poison. Grant knelt down and scooped up a small amount of dirt in his hand. Without thinking twice he placed the dirt on the end of his tongue. It was rough in texture, which was normal, of course. But there was a foul taste that wasn't normal, he spat the dirt out of his mouth. His concerns had been true, the murderer had used a very strong poison in this area.

Another thought occurred in his head, did the killer use this poison on his victim as well? That meant going back to the police station, and have a look at the toxicology report. Something told him that it wouldn't be nearly as easy to get inside as it was last time. Mary wasn't going to be at work this evening, due to their date later that night. Her replacement ended up being an older lady by the name of, Jolene. For some reason that lady hated his guts with a passion, through no fault of his own, of course. Not that she was a bad person Jolene was just very overprotective of, Mary.

Maybe Harris can help me again, Grant thought to himself. “Wouldn't hurt to ask,” Grant mumbled. “Not in the mood to deal with, Jolene.” He reached into his pocket and pulled out his cell-phone. He thumbed through his contacts until he found his friends number and hit the dial sign.

The phone rang several times before Harris answered, “Hello?” By the sound of his voice he was none too happy about being bothered.

“Sorry to bother you again old friend.”

“What do you want now?”

“I need you to let me inside the precinct,” Grant responded. “Jolene is working and you know how she feels about me.”

"I can see how that's a problem for you," Harris said. "Don't ask me to meet you there, I'm busy at the moment and this needs my full attention. Use the Mayor to get you inside." He hung up on him rather quickly.

Grant paced back and forth outside of the police station for a good thirty minutes or so, deciding on if he should walk on inside or not. Captain Simon's wouldn't be happy if she caught him back at the precinct. She allowed him a little time to find that missing girl and nothing more afterward. And if the Mayor was to get a call from the Captain saying he was causing trouble it could end rather bad. Jolene would surely be the one to cause unwanted trouble.

He paced a while longer before making his decision, there was no more time to be wasted. Grant turned to face the doors, straightened his coat and walked inside. He was being stared at by every cop in the building, just like the time before. Some of them admired his tenacity, while others couldn't stand the sight of him.

"Well look what the cat dragged in," Jolene said from behind the counter. "Or should I say puked up."

"Charming as always. Somethings never change."

"Don't be slick with me." Jolene snarled, "I know exactly what kind of man you are, Dawson."

"What did I ever do to make you hate me?"

"You looked at me the wrong way."

Grant smirked, "You're breaking my heart."

"Good. You deserve it after what you did too, Mary."

"What happened between Mary and myself is none of your business!" He shouted.

"You're lucky I'm at work, or I would rip your ass apart." Jolene snarled, "Get out of my sight."

Grant shook his head, "Then unlock the doors behind you, and I will get out of your hair."

She didn't say another word instead of pushing the button and the doors behind her clicked. He made sure not to look back at Jolene as he walked on past right through the double doors. He made his way down the hall with haste, keeping an eye out for Turner, or

Captain Simons. If either one of them caught him back there it could be the last time.

Grant hurried on inside the room where they kept the forensic evidence. He found the file cabinet and began thumbing through them until he found the one he was searching for. He found the toxicology report of the first victim, it was just as he had suspected. The report read that the woman's blood had a foreign substance which could not be analyzed.

"Exactly as I thought. The murderer must have used a certain type of weed killer and mixed it with another type of poison to make it untraceable." To him, it seemed the only way he was going to put all the clues together. Was to find the place that sold strong enough poison that could kill corn stalks.

Exiting the precinct heading for the only place that sold many kinds of farm chemicals. He pulled his car into the parking lot of Bubba's Farming Paradise. He was best friends with the guy that owned the place, or at least he used to be. Things had changed over the past five or six years, so much so that he wasn't sure if he had any friends left in his hometown. Though none of that mattered, Grant was there to investigate not talk with the owner.

As far as the store went, everything seemed to be the same as it was before he left, inside and out. This should be easy enough, Grant thought to himself. Since nothing had changed finding all of the farm chemicals should be a cinch. He walked down to the very back of the store, to the right of him was where his search ended.

Grant browsed through all of the chemicals, reading the ingredients and what each of them does until he came across a certain one. "This one kills almost everything under the sun," Grant whispered to himself. "If I were a betting man this would be the one I would place my money on. But who bought this on the day the first victim disappeared." Grant would have to question the clerk which he did, "My name is Grant Dawson, I'm a private investigator here working a case. I was hoping you could help me out with something."

The clerk was a young man, roughly in his early twenties by his looks he was somewhat of a nerd as well, "Wh-What do you need from me?" He stuttered.

"Calm yourself young man," Grant said. "I just need to ask you a few questions."

The boy smiled nervously, "Okay."

"It has nothing to do with you." Grant reassured him. "What's your name?"

The young man pushed his glasses back up his nose then answered, "Matt."

"Okay, Matt. Were you working here about five years ago?"

Matt thought long and hard, "I believe so."

"What about the day of Halloween?" Grant asked.

"That was my first day working here, I remember it very well."

"Well?"

"A young girl went missing on that day," Matt replied. "At least that was the announcement made on the radio."

"You have a great memory." He was trying to earn the young man's trust by boosting his ego.

Matt snickered, "Well I don't have a four-point grade average in college for nothing."

"Let's test that memory of yours further."

"Challenge accepted."

"See this bag of farm chemical that I'm holding," Grant responded back.

"Yeah, what about it?" Matt replied.

"Did anyone buy this particular bag on that day?"

"Come to think of it, there were three people that bought that bag," Matt responded.

"Who?" Grant asked.

"Bradley Wilson, like always," Matt answered. "Then there was John Davis of course."

"Both farmers," Grant muttered.

"What was that?"

"Nothing. Was there anyone else? Maybe someone that bought a bag of that chemical that didn't seem like they would have a use for it."

"Come to think of it there was a strange lady that bought a bag."

"A lady?" Grant's brow furrowed, "What did she look like?"

"I would say she was about my height, skinny, dressed in black. Umm, I couldn't get a good look at her face though. She kept it hidden behind sunglasses and a hoodie, rarely did she look up at me." Matt explained.

"Did you get a name?" He questioned.

"No, she paid with cash so I couldn't look at her credit card for one."

"Do you have any recordings of that day I can view?" Grant asked.

"Maybe, but you would have to talk with the owner. Even if I knew where they kept them, I couldn't allow you to view the recordings without the owner's permission," Matt told him.

Grant refused to argue with the young man, nor did he try to persuade him either. There was only one way that he could handle the situation without causing an incident. "Here," Grant said, extending a business card to Matt. "Take this and make sure the owner gets it. Have him give me a call as soon as possible tell him it's urgent." He was counting on Bubba to see his name on the card and call him right away.

"Will do, Mr. Dawson," he responded, taking the card from Grant's hand. "Can I ask you something?"

"Sure." Grant nodded.

"These questions you've been asking me." Matt nervously swallowed, "Does it have anything to do with the strange murders?"

He looked at the young man with a stern eye studying his reactions. "Have you ever had any run-ins with the law?"

"Nope, not that I know of."

"Keep it that way." Dawson turned to walk out of the store.

"What about my question!" Matt shouted.

"Just make sure the owner gets that card." Grant waved. Not once did he look back while making his exit out of the building. As Grant was walking in the direction of his vehicle the alarm on his cell-phone went off. He made sure to set the alarm as a reminder of his date with, Mary. This was his way of making sure he didn't forget. He wouldn't get this chance again if he did. Grant rushed back to his hotel room, like a bat out of hell he undressed and jumped into the shower.

After he was done in the shower he speedily dried off with a towel. Grabbed his clothes and got himself dressed, afterward shaving with his electric razor. He put on his tie, threw his blazer over his shoulder and rushed out the door. He didn't know exactly where Mary resided, plus she refused to tell him. So they both agreed to meet, at what was once one of their favorite restaurants.

Later that night he was sitting at the table waiting for his date to arrive. Grant was nervous to the point he wanted to vomit. Most of the time he had nerves of steel, nothing could get to him. He had seen it all, survived everything that was thrown his way, and would come back for more. But the thought of meeting Mary on good terms, made him feel somewhat weak.

When Mary walked inside the restaurant, all eyes shifted to her. She was wearing a red low cut dress that showed off her silky tanned legs. He was taken back after he laid eyes on her, she was just as beautiful as the first time they had met. He took a drink of his wine, then stood up to greet her.

"Mary." Grant smiled, taking her hand in his and kissed the top of it. He pulled the chair away from the table to allow her to sit down.

"Thank you." Mary smiled in return, "I see you haven't lost your charm over the years."

"Not as good as I used to be." Grant laughed. He pulled his chair close to the table and picked up the menu. "Are you hungry?"

"I find that hard to believe." Mary chuckled. "And yes, I could use a bite to eat."

"See anything that interests you?"

"Remember the one meal we used to eat all the time here when we were younger?"

"You had to order the food for both of us because I couldn't pronounce it the right way." Grant had a certain twinkle in his eyes when he spoke, and Mary picked up on that but it only lasted for a brief moment. "Lets order that, it'll be fun."

Mary raised her hand to signal for the waitress, "We're ready to order ma'am," she said. "We shall have the Cannelloni Al Ragu, and another bottle of red wine please."

"Same for both?" The waitress asked.

"Of course." Grant smiled.

She smiled brightly at them both, as she wrote down their orders, "Anything else?"

"No thank you," he replied, handing over the menu.

The waitress looked at Mary, "What about you, Miss?"

Mary smiled, "I'm good."

"Okay," the waitress responded. "I will give your orders to the cook, and have that wine over to you in a jiffy." She smiled at them one more time before rushing away.

As the night went on the two of them talked, mainly about the town and how it hasn't changed a bit. They enjoyed good food, the best wine the town had to offer. Most of all Grant and Mary enjoyed each others company. To them, it was like going back in time when they were young and in love and didn't have a care in the world. Until Mary began to pry into Grant's past, asking questions that he felt should not have been brought up.

"Why didn't we work out, Grant?" Mary's face went from all smiles to a look of seriousness that he was all too familiar with.

"Well, I wanted to move to New York to pursue my career. You, on the other hand didn't want to leave your life behind that you made here." It wasn't the best answer though it was the only one he was willing to give.

"Whatever motivated you to head for New York didn't have anything to do with your career." She wasn't about to take that bullshit excuse he had given her, not then and definitely not now.

"You're right." Grant agreed. "I didn't leave because of my career, I was chasing something much bigger."

Mary shook her head, her eyes filled with sadness for the man she used to know, "You didn't just give chase, you were obsessed to the point that you barely ate, you refused to sleep, and your attitude became unbearable. I know that you wanted to find out what happened to your brother but you let it destroy what you had here."

"What did I have here!" His voice raised. "A dead-end job, or the fact that I lived in a town where everyone looked at me like I was a freak. How about the fact that if I had stayed, I would have never found out what happened to John Boy."

"You had me, Grant! You had me!" Mary replied almost in tears. "And yet you threw me away like my feelings didn't matter like I didn't matter!"

Customers sitting inside the restaurant started to stare at the couple and he quickly picked up on that. "I gave you a chance to come with me," Grant calmly replied.

"And I gave you a chance to stay here with me, to continue our lives together." She took a deep breath to calm herself not wishing to fall apart in front of him.

"I'm sorry that things didn't work out between us," he said.

"After all these years that's all you have to say?!" Mary cried out, getting the attention of a few more dinner patrons. "I loved you! Hell, I still love you damn it!"

"Can we not do this right now people are watching," Grant replied in a colder manner than usual.

"What happened to you?" She sobbed. "What happened to the man that returned my love?"

"The bright-eyed young man that wanted to serve and protect disappeared the day he moved to New York." He ran his fingers through his hair which is one of the nervous habits he tries to hide.

"Look at me and tell me you don't love me." Mary reached out to touch Grant's hand but he quickly pulled away from her.

"A small part of me still loves you," Grant answered. "But you will never find happiness with the man I've become, and I refuse to hurt you again."

She noticed a change in him as the conversation went on. The kind and caring man that she began talking with that night slowly faded into the darkness. Taking his place was a cold and calculated phantom of a person that would stop at nothing to complete the task at hand. She could see that he was right. Grant was not the same man from her past. Still she refused to give up on him, “Why are you hiding your true feelings from me?”

“Let me tell you something about the man sitting in front of you,” Grant said. “He has witnessed horrible things, have fought with demons that you've only seen in your nightmares. Watched one of his good friends die before his very eyes, had to shoot and kill what was once his brother. Going through all of that and more, I'm lucky that I kept my sanity. Yes, I'm a hardass that doesn't give a damn about most people. Be rest assured that I will protect the innocent from crazies like the one in this town.”

Mary took a handkerchief from her purse wiping the tears from her eyes that streamed down her cheeks. “I had no idea you had suffered so much hurt and loss. But that still doesn't change the fact of how I feel about you,” she said.

He dreaded this moment the whole night, somehow he knew it would come, regardless of how hard he fought against it. She had hated his guts since his return into town some umpteen years later. Honestly, he preferred it to be so. Her supposed hatred for him would keep her from trouble, and out of his way. What he didn't expect was for her to ask him out to lunch, which would eventually turn into a late night date. “There's nothing here for you anymore,” he said, talking about himself, of course. “Forget about me and move on with your life.”

The hurt that Mary had felt so many years ago when Grant walked away from her the first time began to resurface. It was a pain that she remembered well and vowed to never feel again. Though here she was, pouring her heart out to a man that no longer cared. Begging him for compassion, pleading with him to understand her. Most of all she was wanting him to love her.

All she could do now was pick herself up, brush her hair out of her face, wipe the tears from her eyes and say the first thing that came to mind. “Maybe you're right,” she responded. “There is nothing left here, I need to move on." She stood from the table, kissed Grant's cheek and began to walk away.

"Stay a little longer." He reached for her but she pulled away.

"I don't think that would be a good idea," she replied, not breaking stride to glance back at him.

Grant stayed behind for an hour or so later, drinking another bottle of wine. He was deep in thought about the offer she had given him. He desperately wanted to tell her how much he loved her, how he had wanted to give their relationship another try. Deep down though, he knew that he could never be happy with leading a normal life. Getting married and having kids was something he once wanted. Until that fateful day he found out the truth about his brother. That changed everything, his whole life had flipped upside down.

His life was one of chaos, booze and cigarettes. On top of that, hunting down what he claimed as "evil beings" and forcing justice upon them was what he craved these days. He stood from his chair and tossed a hundred dollar bill on the table to cover the fee and a tip for the waitress of course. In the act of walking out of the restaurant the hostess stopped him.

"Sir," the man responded.

"What do you want?" Grant questioned. "I paid for the meal now leave me the hell alone."

"It's not that."

"Then what?"

"Is your name, Dawson?" The hostess asked.

Grant glared at the man for a good minute, "Could you be more elaborate? I'm sure there are plenty of men with the last name such as mine."

"I'm sorry." The man nervously smiled, "Grant Dawson. Is that your full name?"

"I am, Grant Dawson. What is it that I can do for you?"

The man held out a folded up piece of paper, "I was asked to give this to you."

"By who?" He asked with a look of bewilderment.

"Some lady." The hostess shrugged.

Maybe this was from, Mary. One last plea for him to focus on their relationship. Or possibly it was going to be a goodbye note, and this would be the last time that she would ever talk to him again. Then again it could be one of those angry letters, that Grant had grown accustomed to. Nevertheless, he had to unfold the paper to find out.

Yet the paper contained none of the above, there was a smiley face staring back at him, winking. Words were written underneath the drawing that read, “you failed her” his hands began to tremble, his face filled with fear. To the point you could see the creases around his eyes and lips with more definition. Though he didn't feel fear for himself, instead he felt it for her.

6

PROMISES NOT THREATS

"WHO GAVE YOU THIS?" GRANT BELTED.

"Like I said, it was some lady," the hostess replied.

"What did she look like?!" He shouted another question at the man.

"I- I don't remember." The hostess frowned.

"Think, damn-it! I need to know and I need to know now!"

"She was wearing all black," the man answered. "Black clothing, shoes, gloves, the works. The lady also had a hoodie covering her face along with a pair of sunglasses."

"Was she with anybody?" Grant questioned.

"Not that I saw, though she was talking with another lady."

"Who?"

"A woman wearing a red dress. They seemed to be having a heated conversation. Then the lady in black walked out, while the other gave chase. About ten minutes later the woman in black came back in and told me to give you this."

Grant rushed out of the restaurant frantically running up and down every street, screaming out Mary's name. Sweat was forming over his brow, his chest was heaving heavily, still yet he ran. He ran until he got to the corner of Fourth and Nickels, where he found one of her high heels laying on the curb. Which in fact confirmed his own suspicions, she had been taken by the murderer. There was nothing more he could do at that point, sure he could call the cops, but that could get her killed. For now it was up to him to figure out a way to save her life. That sure as hell didn't involve help from others.

The night slowly lingered on, he found himself back at his hotel room drinking another bottle of bourbon. Haunted by the thought of what could be happening to Mary, he sat there doing nothing. Images of her being tortured flashed through his head one at a time. If that wasn't enough to drive a man crazy. Then surely the amount of alcohol he was consuming would kill him instead. Grant drank well into the later part of the morning, before passing out on the table.

The sun began to slowly rise as little rays of light shined through the hotel window and down on his face. This act caused him to wake from his slumber. None to worse for wear, Grant made his way to the shower, cleaned himself up, shaved and put on some clean clothing. He fixed himself another glass of bourbon and sat back down at the table. This time around he didn't drink nearly as much. It was as if he was waiting for something or someone.

He sat in his hotel room for most of the day patiently waiting for what he felt would come, and so it did. About four in the afternoon another large yellow envelope was delivered to his room. Though this time it was brought up by the sweet old lady that runs the place. Grant thanked her, and talked with the lady for a good ten minutes, before insisting that he had work to be done.

When he returned to the comfort of his room, Grant immediately opened the envelope. Another tape had fallen out of the package this was no surprise as was the killers M.O. He reached for the cassette player and popped the tape inside pressing the play button. After a brief silence the recording started. Mary's voice was heard first followed by the killer still using that damn voice changing device.

“Someone please help me.” Mary pleaded. “Anyone, anyone at all please help me.”

“Help me. Someone please help me,” the killer mocked just like the last time.

"Who's there?" She shouted. "Help me please. I beg of you."

"I'm not here to help you," the murderer replied. "Neither will anyone else." A muffled noise came next and she could no longer be heard on the recording. "That's better." The killer chuckled. "Let's talk about you, Mr. Dawson. Here again we find ourselves at the end of another one of these bitter discussions. You see, I gave you a chance to leave this town and never or look back. Or the ones you care for would pay the price, yet you refused and I was forced to keep my promise.

Letting you out of town now for the exchange of this young woman's life wouldn't be much fun would it? So allow me to tell you how this is going to go. We're going to play us another fun little game, kind of a catch me if you can sort of deal. The rules are simple, I give you clues you follow my every direction to get these clues. If you refuse to play, nor follow my directions to a tee the girl dies. Play the game and win you save the once love of your life.

You might even get lucky enough to bring me down in the process, who knows. If you ignore me and get the cops involved, well you get the picture by now. Let's play, shall we? The first part of the game starts right now. Find the key that I hid in your vehicle, figure out where it goes and you will have what you need to progress. Oh, and good luck." The tape ended there.

Grant didn't give it a second thought, he rushed out of the hotel in the direction his vehicle was parked. His hands trembling with the uncertainty of finding a key or not. What didn't cross his mind at the time was the thought of how the murderer got into the locked vehicle in the first place. He destroyed the inside of his car looking for the object in question. Grant was a man possessed, he was throwing things out into the parking lot making a big mess. By the time he was done he had pretty much ripped the whole inside from the vehicle.

The man was pissed-off that his search proved fruitless. And began to wonder if this wasn't the murderer's way of playing sick mind games with him. That is until he caught a glimpse of something that looked like it had been taped underneath the dashboard. Grant reached for the object and removed it from its hiding place. It was indeed the key he had been searching for all along, but what does it go to?

The thoughts that ran through his head wasn't pleasant ones, he knew where this key belonged. What would he find on the other side of the door he had to unlock. Could be possible that there would be another dead body waiting to be discovered, maybe even Mary's. Or perhaps the crazed maniac set up something more sinister for him to find. Although none of that mattered, he had to play the killers sick and twisted game if he wanted to save Mary's life.

He jumped into the driver's seat and started the car. He needed to go to Leonard Clifton's apartment. He drove through town with a lead foot, not bothering with speed limits. His vehicle came to a screeching halt when he found a parking spot. Grant wanted to rush inside the apartment, though that would draw unwanted attention. Not that speeding through town wasn't enough to do the trick.

With the thought of not drawing unwanted eyes his way, Grant casually walked inside the building. He had a quickness to his step, with a stern look on his face that turned the slightest eye. He was clearly a man on a mission, not a soul would keep him from what had to be done. He walked up the steps then made his way down the hallway towards Clifton's apartment.

Again he found himself standing outside of the apartment door. He reached for the handle and indeed the door had been locked. The doorknob looked brand new like it had just recently been changed. Which would make sense, seeing how the last time he was there he himself kicked the door in. How did the killer get his or her hands on the new key to this particular door?

The thought of the killer being a woman crossed his mind as well. That wouldn't be too outlandish, he has run across many crazed ladies that would kill if necessary. Though the murderer claimed to be a man at first, could very possibly be a woman. Since this woman in black has been popping up everywhere the killer had been. Not to mention she was seen talking with Mary before she disappeared.

Thoughts were thoughts, and that's just what they were at the moment. He placed the key in the lock and turned it with the slightest movement of the wrist. The lock clicked and the door opened. He cautiously made his way inside, just in case it was a trap. The room looked normal, more than likely for the first time clean. He searched the apartment thoroughly and came up empty-handed. What in the hell am I supposed to find here? Grant thought to himself. There's not a bloody thing and I've been searching for a damn hour.

A foul stench began to fill the air, which drew his attention back to the task given to him. He followed the smell around the apartment, it was an all to a familiar odor that was recognized right away. It was the smell of death, rotten, stinking, death. That foul odor lead him straight to the kitchen sink.

The smell is coming from under the sink, Grant knelt down reaching out to open the cabinet doors. He shook his head and snarled at the sight of the item left for him by the killer. He was looking straight at some poor souls heart, a dried up bloodless heart. And if he was a guessing man, he would say this was Leonard Clifton's missing heart.

When he picked the heart up in his hands, there was a note attached, "Break my heart and see what's inside." Grant didn't like the idea of ripping the heart in half, but if this was the only way to proceed then the hell with it. Plunging his thumb and forefinger straight into the heart, though it was dry it was still squishy in his hands. He smashed and tore at the organ until his fingers felt something hard with a plastic texture.

He got to his feet and bumped the sink handle on with his elbow. Proceeding to wash the remains of the heart down the drain. As the dried clumped up blood, along with the pieces of the heart went down the drain, in this nasty, grotesque swirl of water. Grant began to wonder about what sort of object he held. Before long the only thing left in his hand was a sim card for a cell phone his cell phone to be exact.

He didn't want to place the sim card in his phone while inside the apartment. Once he got back inside his car, Grant placed the item in his phone. The screen went fuzzy, the phone shut itself off for a few minutes. When the device turned back on everything was different. The screen saver had changed to a picture of a dead body with two files for him to select, pictures and messages.

Making the decision to look at the pictures first, he tapped the screen with his thumb and random photos appeared. The first picture set his anger boiling over, it was of Mary she had been bound and gagged. He could see the fear in her eyes as that picture had been taken. There were two more pictures of her. This was the killer's way of letting him know that she still lived. He backed out of the pictures and clicked on the file that said “messages.” At first there was nothing, no sound no white-noise nothing at all. Out of the blue a different voice than what he was used to began to talk.

“Hello, Mr. Dawson.” It was the voice of a female, not the usual distorted voice he had grown accustomed to, “Bet you didn't expect to hear a female talking did you.” She chuckled lightly, “Let’s get down to business. You have something he wants, you're probably wondering what that is.” That part was true, he had no idea what item she could be referring to. “I'm going to elaborate, the files that you carry he wants them. You see those files have too much information. He doesn't want those said files floating around out there. He also doesn't want them to stay in your hands either.

Listen closely, this is what you are going to do next. Go back to your hotel room, gather those files then head for the corner of Hamilton and Main. He tells me there is a small burger joint at that very spot. Where you and your brother loved to hang out as kids. When you arrive, place the files in the garbage can out front. Don't try any funny business or he will know, then your girly friend will die. Consider that as me being nice, giving you a warning in advance.

After you have made the drop, go inside and grab a bite to eat god knows you look like you need one. Stay inside for a good hour at least, and who knows, maybe you will get a nice little gift if all goes well.” Laughter ensued signaling the end of the recording.

Dawson muttered a few curse words under his breath and shoved his phone back in his pocket. He reached out placing the keys in the ignition, started the engine, pulled the gear shift in reverse and stomped the gas pedal hard with his foot. The vehicle bolted backward like it had been shot out of a cannon. Putting the gear shift into drive and stomped the pedal again. The wheels spun, smoke erupted out of the back of the vehicle before it flew down the highway like a bat out of hell.

Within no time he had made it to the destination he was instructed to be with the files. He grabbed the items, jumped out of the vehicle doing as he was told. After dropping the files in the trash can he slowly walked inside the burger joint making sure not to look back. If anyone caught him taking the slightest peek, it could put Mary's life in even more danger.

This old diner that Grant found himself standing inside of brought back some joyful yet painful memories. He remembered the burger joint well. And why would he not? It was the place that he and his brother loved the most as kids. For the first time in a long while a smile crept across his face. And not one of those fake smiles he was so used to giving people this was sincere.

Not much had changed, the white metal bar tables with the wood grain tops still filled the room. With the old-timey chairs neatly tucked underneath. As always you could see the cooks in the kitchen working endlessly to get the orders of food out to the customers. That sweet aroma of french fries and onion rings, along with greasy meat saturated the entire dinner.

The only difference between then and now was the person that owned the joint. Old man Simpson had owned the place for over forty years like his father before him and his father before him. When old man Simpson passed away, God rest his soul, he didn't have any children to pass the family business down to. And it went to the banks then straight to the auction house. Last he heard, a man by the name of Bradley Smith bought the place. The townsfolk insisted he kept everything the same to honor the Simpsons for all they've done. Smith, not being a stupid man did as asked of him to keep the place thriving, it of course worked in his favor.

Grant took a seat at a table placed in the far back corner, he wanted to stay away from the other patrons. If someone recognized him and started a conversation, it would only enrage him further. In a split second a waitress was at his table ready to take his order.

"What can I get you today, sir?" She asked.

The table was already set up with a menu to browse, but there was no need. He knew what he wanted without giving it a second thought. "Yes, ma'am. I will take a double-bacon-cheeseburger, medium well, with a side of fries," he said.

"What to drink?"

"One of that famous root-beers will work just fine."

What Grant wanted badly was a couple of shots of bourbon, that wasn't going to happen at this dinner. They didn't believe in selling booze at their establishment. Drunks were not the type of people that would help food sales. If anything it would drive away the good customers.

Fifteen minutes later the waitress returned with his food and drink. The meal before him looked delicious, the wondrous aroma of the french fries. The sizzling of the grease as is dripped off the freshly cooked hamburger meat and onto his plate was enough to make him salivate. For a brief moment he forgot that the waitress was standing beside him.

"Can I get you anything else?" Looking as though she might laugh at the man before her for the way he stared at the cheeseburger.

"No thank you."

"Enjoy," she politely replied, then walked back towards the other patrons leaving him to enjoy his meal.

Scooping up the double-bacon-cheeseburger with both hands, drool was forming on both sides of his mouth. He took a big bite out of the burger, reached down to take a handful of fries to shove in his mouth. His appetite had returned with a vengeance. After days of doing nothing more than drinking bourbon for two days, his body craved food and he had no choice but to oblige. Grant took no time in obliterating his food one quick bite after another.

What he hadn't noticed was the audience in the room watching him scarf down his food like a man starving to death. When he was done eating, he gulped down his root beer in one foul swoop. Grant put his empty glass back down on the table, immediately upon looking back up for the waitress he had noticed that the diner had emptied. There was not one person there except for himself. The patrons before him were gone, the staff that worked there had also vanished.

"Hello? Is anyone there?" He called out. He waited then called out again, "Can I get my check please, I'm ready to leave." Where did everyone go? Did I stay past close by accident? He thought to himself.

"Nobody here but us little brother." It wasn't that of an adults voice but of a young child.

"Show yourself kid!" Grant demanded.

A figure slowly walked out of the shadows, to his horror it was his older brother, John Boy. This though was not the John Boy from Grant's memories but of his nightmares. The child was wearing a hospital gown, his skin was a pasty white, his eyes were sunk deep into his sockets. But nothing compared to seeing the bullet hole in John Boy's forehead where blood and pus oozed out.

"This can't be real!" Grant gasped. He closed his eyes rubbing on his temples, "You're not real!" When there was no shuffling of the feet, nor words being spoken. Thinking for sure his hallucination had passed he opened his eyes and seen John Boy face to face, nose to nose with him. He screamed and damn near stumbled over backwards in his chair.

"You're a funny little brother." John Boy chuckled.

"You're not real!" He screamed again, slamming his fists on the table.

The boy cracked a smile, revealing his nasty rotting yellow teeth, "Then what am I?" Blood trickled down off his face and onto the table. The sound of the blood dripping on the table reminded Grant of a leaky faucet. "Well, I'm waiting."

"You're a figment of my imagination. Brought on by sleepless nights and bourbon." Grant hissed.

John Boy started to laugh, as if Grant had told the funniest joke he had ever heard, "Truth be told little brother, I am the ghost that will haunt you for the rest of your miserable life." His smile turned into a grimace of disgust.

"Why? What did I ever do to you?"

"Did you forget that you yourself put this bullet between my eyes." The boy pointed to the hole in his forehead, "You did this to me, little brother! It was your gun that killed me! You killed me!"

"You were already dead!" Grant screamed back at him. But John-Boy was gone and the diner had returned to normal. The patrons stared at him like he was a madman talking to himself. He could hear them whispering to each other, he had frightened them that much was clear. He gave a faint smile to reassure the customers that everything was fine. But his smile was twisted, shaky and downright creepy. The ones that didn't get up to leave stayed behind only to finish their food.

"Sir, are you okay?" The waitress walked up and asked.

Beads of sweat were forming on his forehead his hands were trembling and wet from perspiration. "I'm fine, just a bad dream. Sorry about that I didn't mean to fall asleep."

"Sir, you were awake the whole time," she replied. "Mumbling to yourself for the longest before shouting aloud and hitting the table with your fists. You've scared many of the customers out of here."

"Would you like for me to leave?"

The waitress nervously smiled, most of the time when she asks a customer to leave they tend to get upset with her. But the man before her was mostly in a state of panic and to her mildly crazy to boot. Not the usual town drunks that she had grown accustomed to. "That would be for the best," she said.

"Get my check ready and I will be out of your hair."

"I already have it ready for you." She set his bill on the table and hurried away like a rat being chased by a cat.

Grant looked at the check, took a couple of the twenties out of his wallet placing them on the table to cover the bill and a tip for the young lady. He grabbed his coat then made his way out of the diner. Hopefully, it has been over an hour, I have no choice but to walk outside now. I didn't realize that I was going to have a nervous breakdown in there, scaring the hell out of everyone, he thought.

Walking over to the garbage can where he placed the files. He glanced inside, the files had been taken and replaced with another item. It was a small grey ring case, he reached for the item and picked it up. For a brief moment, he had second thoughts about opening the case. The last time he had opened one of those he found a pinky finger inside. God knows Grant would lose it if one of Mary's fingers laid inside this little box. He grimaced and opened the box regardless. What he found inside was not a finger just another sim card for his phone. He let out a sigh of relief, then closed the box and shoved it into his pants pocket.

Though he still stood there, as if there was one more thing he had to do before his legs would allow him to leave. Grant gazed at his old beaten brown trench coat that was draped over his forearm. Like it was some sort of foreign object.

“Why do I still hang onto this thing?” He muttered under his breath. I know why he thought. It's my safety net. A way of hiding my true self. I put this coat on and pretend to be someone else, someone that I'm not. Makes it easier this way, easier to accept what I've become over the years.

When I'm this other person I gain trust with ease, I don't have to fight much. In the end it's my darker half that gets the job done. And right now, I need to be that man that will do anything it takes to solve this case. That will do anything and everything to save Mary's life, even if I have to take a life or hand out swift justice.

He tossed the coat into the garbage can, “I'm tired of playing nice, tired of hiding behind this mask.” He took a pack of smokes and matches out of his shirt pocket. Placed the butt end of a cigarette in his mouth, struck a match and lit up a cigarette. Grant took a long drag off his cigarette exhaling a thick cloud of smoke afterward. He held the burning end of the match underneath the book of matches setting them ablaze. Grant took another drag from his cigarette and tossed the burning matches into the garbage can. His coat went up in flames, signifying a new beginning.

7

TRIALS TO OVERCOME

THE DAY WAS SLOWLY COMING TO AN END, THE SUN WAS BEGINNING TO set, and night would soon be upon the town of Dover. Parents at this time would be making their kids clean up for supper. While the older gents are preparing to hunker down for the night. With the murders occurring more frequently, the people of Dover's nerves have been up, tensions have been running high. When the sun goes down, most of the residents are locked up in their homes by their own free will.

Grant sat in his vehicle with his phone in one hand and a bottle of bourbon in the other. He was drinking just enough to take the edge off of the tension building in his body. He had just listened to his next set of instructions and wasn't sure how to take it. He was instructed to wait until midnight, then drive out to the abandoned shoe factory, the killer was sure he knew the one.

The murderer was right at that, he knew of the old shoe factory that sat thirty-five miles outside of town. It was a staple of the town for over fifty years. Until one night a fire broke out inside the factory killing everyone inside. After that nightmare ended the people of Dover turned a blind eye to what happened that night. Nowadays the citizens act as though the shoe factory never existed.

Grant drove thirty miles out, it was a long rough drive. The road that leads out to the factory had potholes around every corner. It was dark with very little light. The wind was howling, making it hard for him to see because of the blowing dust. Light from the full moon offered very little comfort making the shoe factory look ominous from a distance.

The vehicle's headlights revealed a large steel fence that went all away around the factory as it approached. He was going to have to park the car and find a way inside. Which meant he would have to walk the rest of the distance. He found a place to hide his car and turned off the ignition, he reached into the back seat grabbing his bag. Grant had prepared for anything, the bag was packed with a flashlight, first aid kit, a taser along with a couple of handguns just in case.

He flung the bag over his shoulder walking over to the steel fence. He used his flashlight to take a closer look at the rusty old fence before him. I could climb over, he thought. When he shined his light towards the top, he knew right then it would be a bad idea. At the top were rolls of barbed wire that would rip his pants and flesh to shreds.

Looks like I have to find another way in, Grant walked along the fence line hoping that he would find where the fence had been cut or maybe torn down. There had to be a way through seeing how this was the hangout for junkies and teens that wanted to get drunk without being seen. He happened upon a spot where the ground had been disturbed and covered with random garbage. No surprise that a trench had been dug underneath the fence. But you couldn't find it unless you were looking hard enough.

Figures that I would have to dig under the fence like a dog trying to get into the next door neighbors yard, Grant frowned at this thought. He tossed his bag up and over the fence landing it right in front of him on the other side. He got down on his hands and knees clearing the trash and debris away from the fence. When he was done with that he began to dig his way underneath.

He pushed all the dirt to the side and squeezed his body under the fence, pulling himself through and out on the other side. Grant dusted the dirt off his shirt and pants, spate the dirt out of his mouth, and once again threw his bag over his shoulder. He took his flashlight out and turned it on, using the light to make his way towards the factory.

The building was dark and ominous up close. Half of the shoe factory was still black from the fire, the windows were broken and boarded up. It looked like the place was on lockdown. Except one place on the building wasn't nailed shut. "Seems this is where I am supposed to go." He placed his bag on the ground, pulled the zipper back and retrieved one of his guns. He kicked the door open with the gun straight out in front of him, slowly walking inside. He was prepared for anything the murderer could throw at him. At least that is what he thought until he made his way further inside.

Someone has been busy, Grant thought. There was one path for the man to take, straight ahead. Walls had been put up on both sides, which was not apart of the original design. The walk space was narrow with very little room to turn, strange symbols along with words that could not read had been painted on the walls in red. This kind of work would have taken years for one man to do on his own. That lead him into believing the killer had planned this for a long time. And he was lucky enough to be the first participant.

Grant followed down the narrow path until he came to a dead end. It wasn't one of those times where he had to turn around and go back the way he came. There on the wall was a small opening, he assumed it was just big enough for him to fit his body into. To make it more obvious that this was the direction he was meant to go in. An arrow had been painted above pointing down at the square hole with words saying, "Crawl for your woman."

This was not something he was expecting out of the murderer. Everything Grant was seeing was well thought out and planned ahead of time. Not something a man going out of his mind would do so easily, or willingly. No, it was clear the killer was smart, not crazy as he had assumed. All of this had a meaning, or a means to an end. The only way to find out what that ending had in store for him, would be to finish what had been started.

He dropped his bag to the ground, knelt down beside it, reached out and unzipped the bag. He pulled out a couple of guns and stuck them snug in his back gun holsters. Grant also grabbed a few clips of ammo, and batteries for the flashlight placing those in his pockets. That was all he could carry if he was going to fit into that tiny crawl space. He took off his jacket and tossed it to the side before squeezing his upper body into the crawl space.

He wiggled his way down the ventilation duct until he came to a spot where he had to make a choice, left or right. He was certain that if he took the wrong path the outcome would be death. An idea sprang into his mind. Grant could barely maneuver in the tight space, yet still managed to get to his shirt pocket to retrieve a book of matches. He took a single match out of the box. With a quick motion struck the match causing the end to flame up.

Using the flame off the match should show him which direction he needed to crawl in. It was simple science if there was an exit out of the crawl space. Air would flow through the vent towards that very exit, pulling the flame in that direction. Sure as shit the flame pulled towards the right. He blew out the match, thumped it out in front of him, and started to crawl again. As he made his way further down the vent duct, Grant felt sharp pains up his forearms and legs. Even though the pain was unbearable, he pressed on.

The small crawl space was hot to the point that his clothing was wet from sweat. Not only that, he could feel another warm liquid running down his arms and legs to go along with the pain and heat. He wanted out of the vent duct just as badly as he wanted to save, Mary. His head was swimming, and his whole body ached.

On top of that, it was so humid he could barely breathe. When he thought he was getting close to the exit, another fork in the road appeared. He went through the same procedure as before, except this time he caught a glimpse of what he had been crawling on top of. It was broken glass for christ sake, it was broken glass that was tearing his flesh to shreds.

Blood was trickling down his arm onto the shiny surface underneath him. Grant looked at his forearms and there were chunks of glass that had dug into his skin. He was so hell-bent on getting out of that tiny space, that he never noticed the glass until now. There was no time to waste on pulling out the glass, he would just end up with more in his flesh anyways before making it out. He did the only thing he could do, he pressed on. He crawled on the broken glass for a while longer, wondering if the madness would ever end.

While he was crawling onward, something unexpected happened. The vent duct gave way, and he fell a good five feet before hitting the ground with a hard thud. Grant laid on his back looking up at the rusty steel beams that were holding the shoe factory. He was breathing heavily and his left leg was killing him, if his leg was broken, he would be in a hell of a lot of trouble. It took all the strength he had to pull himself to his feet. His leg was hurt, luckily not broken. Grant pulled the glass from his arms, and what he could get from his legs, even his stomach had glass shards to remove.

His shirt and jeans had been ripped to shreds, something he would have to take care of later. He had hoped that the worst was over, but it wasn't, the fun was just getting started. After he gathered his thoughts, Grant turned to see that another (not so fun) game awaited him. Wires ran from one wall to the other, in rows of four. It wasn't barbed wire, no that would be too easy.

Grant knew that the fence was electrical by the way the wires were set up. Maybe I can pass this game up altogether, Grant thought after he spotted the door off to the side. He wasted no time in hurrying over to the steel door, though a little voice in his head was telling him, (this is to easy.) As he approached there was a note taped to the door with his name on it. He reached out and yanked the note down and opened it. The note read like this, "Go through this door, and Mary dies. Stay, play, and win. You will be one step closer to saving her life. Have fun!" It ended with a smiley face drawn on the paper.

Becoming irate he ripped the note in half throwing it to the ground, yelling curse words the whole time. He was tired, sweaty, and bleeding, his body ached with pain, he was beginning to come unglued. "I have to calm down." Taking a couple of deep breaths. "If I lose my cool here then I die." He closed his eyes, took in another deep breath, and prepared himself for what must be done next. He made his way over to where the wires were placed.

"I have to find out how much current is running through these wires." Grant grabbed at one of the strands. A bright flash followed by extreme pain was all he that he remembered happening next. The wires had enough electricity running through them that it burned the palm of his hand and almost knocked him out. Say he were to do that to many times it would kill him, likely by stopping his heart.

He studied his surroundings by walking from wall to wall, staring at the wires the whole time. Trying to figure out a way to survive the torturous test ahead. There had to be a way to get through the crazy maze without getting shocked. After several minutes of relentlessly staring at those blasted wires, Grant finally figured it out. A space in between one section of the copper wires was just wide enough for him to duck under if he was careful. He put his right leg out under the wire, slowly worked his head and torso underneath, stood up pulling his left leg under and out.

"Damn, that was close," Grant muttered, wiping the sweat from his forehead. He started the task over again, finding the way through the next round of wires that stood in front of him and the exit. This time the way to the other side was closer to the ground, which meant he was probably going to be shocked. Again he put his right leg under the wire, crouched as low as he could go, and under the wire he went. He barely touched the wire, pain shot through his leg and up his back. Lucky it wasn't enough to stop him or make him pass out. He did have to take a breather to regain his composure.

Grant would have to search again for a way past the next set of wires. He found what he was looking for, there was another gap in the wires, this time it was close to the top. Not going to be so easy this time around, he thought to himself. He would have to get somewhat of a running start and jump through the gap. That was the only option left to him if he miscalculated by just a little. Grant would fall on the electric fence and would surely perish.

It's now or never, he readied himself, took a couple of deep breaths, and off he went. He didn't have much room to get a good start, still he had to try. Once close enough he jumped, stretched out his body, arms and head first, with his feet last to land on the ground. Grant made it to the other side without incident. He jumped to his feet, dusted himself off, and wanted to cheer for making it through alive. But he had one more hurdle to cross, or crawl under that is. It didn't take long for him to find the way through the last set of wires that awaited him. He was going to have to crawl underneath to make it to the other side.

"Why would the killer make the last one this easy?" Grant whispered. "This doesn't make any sense." While he was questioning if he should go any further, screams of fear found its way to his ears. "Mary! Mary! It's me, Grant! I'm here to help!" With haste he started to crawl under the wires, he was in such a panic that he never realized his back was touching the electric fence. The pain was intense, but the need to get to Mary made him numb to everything.

His shirt was smoking, while the flesh on his back was burning. Still, he managed to get underneath. When he got to his feet he was weak, barely able to stand. Grant stumbled forward towards where the screaming was coming from. There were steps leading down into the basement area of the shoe factory, he stumbled his way down them one at a time. Before he could get to the bottom step, his knees buckled and he went rolling down the last four steps.

Hurt and slightly embarrassed, Grant reached up grabbing the railing to pull himself to his feet. He was getting closer to where the screaming was coming from. Again he stumbled on using the wall to hold himself steady, if not for that he wouldn't be able to walk. Though he wasn't sure what to think when he found where the screaming had been coming from.

It was just a tape recording playing over and over again. He walked over and picked up the tape player, "Son of a bitch!" He threw the device against the wall, shattering it on contact. "Where is, Mary?" Grant shouted. "Where is she you sick son of a bitch!" He fell to his knees, his body was starting to give out. He tried to get back to his feet but his legs were like jelly and he went down face first on the floor. Thoughts of Mary went blazing through his head, he felt like he had let her down. Something in the pit of his stomach told him he was going to die here, and she would be left to the will of the murderer. “I’m sorry, Mary. I’m-” His eyes closed, darkness surrounded him.

8

MORE BAD DREAMS

"WAKE UP, GRANT." HE OPENED HIS EYES TO SEE MARY STANDING OVER him smiling.

"Where am I?" He groggily asked.

"You're home silly." Mary laughed. "Where do you think you are?"

"How?"

She bent over and kissed Grant's lips, "You must have had another one of your dreams."

"Must have." He gave a confused smile, as he wasn't sure of what was happening. It must be a dream he was stuck in, last he remembered was the feeling of fading away on the floor of the shoe factory. Or perhaps he was dead, and this was heaven, or possibly hell. All he knew was that he woke up in his old bed and house with Mary by his side.

"Are you going to get up or stay in bed all day?" She giggled. "Or did you forget what today is?"

"Rough night, my mind is somewhat foggy." Grant smiled, crawling out of bed. "Mind filling in the gaps?"

"We're getting married next week. Today is the day you go find a tux and I look for a wedding dress with my family and friends. I would be so mad at you if I didn't love you so much."

"Then I better hurry." He played along but something didn't feel right. We were never engaged, I thought about before I got that lead about my older brother. "You know I love you right?"

She turned back to face him, "You're acting weird today, is something wrong?" She asked not once taking her eyes off him.

Grant frowned and said, "We were never engaged. This never happened, I must be dreaming or dying."

"Why say such hurtful things?" Tears began to well up in her eyes, "Do you not love me or are you getting cold feet?"

"I love you. I swear to god I do, but this isn't real. The day that I was going to ask for your hand in marriage, was the day I got a phone call that changed everything. A detective that I had been talking with found more information on my brother. I was told that he could still be alive after all these years of being told that he was dead.

The only way I could know for sure was to join the ranks of the N.Y.P.D. When I told you what I wanted to do and offered for you to come with. We fought, probably one of the worst fights we ever had. You told me to make a choice, chase after the past or make a future with you. I left for New York the next day by myself. You know, I can accept my fate for what I have done. Have I forgiven myself? No, but I can accept it. But I will never be able to rest in peace if I stay here and let Mary die for real."

"Why not?" She smiled. "All you have to do is think about your happiness for once. Stay here with me, be happy. What do you say?"

"I'm sorry, there's no way I can do that," he said.

She lowered her head and began to laugh, "It's funny that you think you have a choice." She lunged at him grabbing for his shoulders, her face changed shape as she laughed on like a wild crazed animal. Grant watched terrified as Mary's flesh was melting off. What was left was the face of his older brother, John Boy. He fought with the grip of whatever had him, but couldn't break free, he had to watch his dead brother laugh in his face.

Until this monstrous thing before him took another shape, the face of Billy, a man from his past appeared before him. Then it took another face, Bobby, another man from his past, next it was Tommy, like the others he knew that man as well. Last was the burnt face of Albert, a monster of a man that enjoyed taking innocent lives. It was those other men, and Grant himself that ended Albert's reign of terror, and it cost them all dearly.

"Miss me?" Albert growled. "I've missed you."

"We killed you!" Grant screamed out.

"Are sure about that?" Albert smiled, showing his razor-sharp teeth.

In the back of Grant's mind, it was clear that none of this was real. Though it sure as hell felt like it was when Albert began to choke the life out of him. He was a fighter and did all he could to break free, but the fight in him was fading fast. His breathing was shallow, he could feel the last bit of strength slipping away. His thoughts went straight to Mary, I'm sorry, Mary. I didn't want it to end this way, I should have never come back here.

"Grant! Grant!" A voice called out in the distance. "Damn it, don't die on me! Don't you dare die on me!"

That voice sounds familiar to me, Grant thought. Suddenly, it was like a light went off in his head, Harris was the one yelling at him, trying to get him to fight for his life. "You will never escape your past, no matter how hard you try. The memories will haunt you until the day you die." Albert laughed.

"I can live with that. It's the nightmares like you that keep me going." He sat straight up gasping for air he was damn lucky to be alive, surviving the torture chamber.

"Thank god you're alive." Harris sighed.

Grant coughed, "How did you find me anyways?"

"Got a call about a prowler out this way," he answered. "Didn't expect to find you out here barely alive. What in the hell is all of this?"

"Nothing important." He shrugged, holding out his hand, "Help me up will you."

Harris took his hand and pulled him to his feet, "Is that all you have to say?"

"Pretty much."

"Enough with the bullshit. Look at you, you can barely stand. Your shirt and jeans are ripped to shreds, you have burns and cuts all over your body. Not to mention your bleeding, face it you look like shit. Again, cut the crap and tell me what's going on."

"Don't worry about it." Grant went to walk away, Harris stopped him in his tracks by grabbing his arm, "Let me go."

"Let me help you, you know you can trust me."

Grant pulled his arm free of Harris's grip, "You can't help me now no-one can."

"I can place you under arrest if need be." Harris warned him.

Grant held his arms out in front of him with his wrists together, "Then do it." Lieutenant Harris hesitated, "What are you waiting for?"

He couldn't arrest his friend, not here, not now. "Just go! Before I change my mind."

"Look, there's nothing you can do to help. I'm already too far gone."

He turned his back to Harris and walked away. Harris was smiling at Grant, watching him leave, there was something evil in that smile, something dangerous.

9

THINGS THAT CHANGE A MAN

LIEUTENANT HARRIS SAT AT HIS DESK BACK AT THE PRECINCT, HIS GAZE was squarely upon a picture of a middle-aged lady, standing next to her was a young girl. He reached out picking the picture up, bringing it closer to his face. “Francis, how I’ve missed you.” A faint smile crossed his lips. “After Christy died, we were never the same. I remember it like it was yesterday, some memories never fade, they only make you see the world for what it truly is.”

It was Thanksgiving day, cold and snowing, Christy was on her college break making her way home. While Harris and his wife Francis were home cooking the turkey and all the fixings. They were both ecstatic that their daughter was coming home for the holidays. It had been half a year since the last time they had seen her. When the time came, family members from both sides poured through the doors. With only one person missing, Christy.

“Where do you suppose Christy is at dear?” Francis asked.

“She said she was in town the last time she called,” he answered.

“I’m worried.” She frowned, “It’s not like her to be late.”

“She’s a big girl now hun. Christy can take care of herself, I’m sure she will be here soon.”

"I hope you're right," she responded. There was something in her voice that gave her husband the chills.

An hour went by and still no word yet from, Christy. Harris had a mound of food on the table in front of him, like every year before. Yet he had hardly touched his plate. When he looked over at his wife, she was laughing and talking with the rest of the family. She was putting on a brave face yet her eyes told him a different story. Francis had the look of a mother worried for her child, those eyes pleaded with him to call anyone and everyone that could give them both relief. He nodded to her, then excused himself from the table. He was going to give his boys a call down at the precinct to see if they could help him find his missing daughter.

Harris walked into the living room of his house for some privacy. The phone began to ring, it looked like he wouldn't get the chance to make that call after all. He had a feeling that it wouldn't be necessary anyway. Harris picked up the phone holding it to his ear, "Harris residence."

"Dan this is Paul. We need to talk."

"You know that I'm not on call tonight, right Paul?"

"It's about your daughter," Paul said.

"Funny you should bring that up, I-" Harris began.

"She's been in an accident, Dan." Paul interrupted. The conversation had suddenly gone quiet, "Did you hear? Your daughter is hurt badly, Dan. Get Francis, and get your asses to the hospital. Do you understand me?"

Francis walked into the room just as Dan was hanging up the phone. By the look on his face, immediately she could tell that something was wrong. "Dan? What's going on? Who was that on the phone? Was it, Christy?"

"Grab your coat, we need to get to the hospital!" Dan said with urgency.

On the way to the hospital, Francis was in a panic fearing the worst. There was only one person that could calm those fears, "Dan, who called? Please tell me, I don't think I can take any more of not knowing." She pleaded.

"Paul called," Harris answered grimly.

"What did he want?" Dan ignored the question keeping his eyes on the road. "Dan please!" Her voice pleading, shaky, seeking comfort from her husband.

"Christy was in an accident," he answered in a low voice.

"Oh god!" Francis cried out. "How bad was it?"

"Paul didn't say."

The vehicle flew into the parking lot of the hospital at an insanely high speed. Dan slammed the brakes and the vehicle skidded into a parking spot, he jerked the gear shaft to park. Francis flung the passenger side door open, running straight for the hospital entrance with Dan hot on her heels.

"Where is my baby! She's here, I know she's here!" Francis shouted in a panicked state of mind.

"Ma'am, you need to calm yourself," one of the nurses said. "You're scaring the other patients."

Dan came running up, "Our daughter has been in an accident, we were told that she was taken here," he said.

"What is her name?" the nurse asked.

"Christy Harris," Dan replied, trying to hide the panic in his voice.

The nurse turned to look at the lady working the receptionist desk, "Nancy would you be so kind as to tell these two if their daughter was brought in or not."

"Of course. What is her name?"

"Christy Harris."

The receptionist typed away on her keyboard for a moment, "Donna would you come here for just a second." Her face had turned pale, it was clear she didn't want to answer the question out loud.

Donna smiled at Dan and Francis, "I will be right back, I promise we will get you to where you need to be." Whispering ensued between Donna and Nancy which seemed to draw the ire of Harris and his wife.

"Would someone please tell me where our daughter is at!" Dan shouted.

"You two follow me," Donna called to them both. She led them down the hall and into an empty waiting room, "Have a seat here, the doctor will be with you shortly."

"Please tell us what is going on!" Dan pleaded. "Can't you see what this is doing to my wife?"

Donna sighed, "I think it would be for the best if I let the doctor speak with you." She gave a half-hearted smile, then walked away.

Not long after Donna parted ways, the doctor walked into the room, "Are you Mr. and Mrs. Harris?"

"We are." Francis was sobbing uncontrollably.

"Will you tell us what in the hell is going on around here?" Dan insisted.

"Your daughter was hit by a drunk driver when walking out of the local gas station. She has sustained multiple injuries to her legs, arms, and torso. Worst of all she has suffered a brain injury," the doctor explained.

"You're lying to us!" Francis cried out, nearly taking a swing at the doctor if Dan hadn't stopped her.

"It's okay. It's going to be okay," Dan said, holding onto Francis tightly. "Doctor, is Christy going to be alright?

The doctor shook his head, "It's not that simple, Mr. Harris. Christy's brain is hemorrhaging blood. Right now we have her in a coma induced sleep, but she needs to have surgery. Until the bleeding stops, there's nothing more we can do. The staff here has made her as comfortable as possible, I will have the nurse take you to her soon. This is the part of my job that I hate, but I have to be honest with you both. The odds of your daughter making it through the rest of the week are slim. Though I assure you we are doing all that we can, you have my sympathy."

For the remainder of that night, the Harris's stayed at the hospital with their daughter. Francis was at the hospital every day with Christy, taking her things from the house, along with fresh flowers to brighten up the room. Dan tried his best to be there as much as he could, though his job took up most of his time. On the fifth day, while Dan was working on a major case, Christy passed away. He felt so much guilt, and the pain he was feeling could not be put into words.

Three weeks after Christy's funeral, Francis passed away in the same hospital as her daughter. Doctors said she had died of a heart attack from all of the stress she had put her body through over the weeks. But Dan knew better, his wife had died from a broken heart over losing their only child. This loss sent Dan over the edge, he demanded that the precinct do something about his daughter's death. When his demands were ignored, he took matters into his own hands. Dan went to arrest the driver responsible for his daughter's death, Jake White.

The precinct had other plans, they stopped him before he could do something stupid. They also warned him that if he tried anything like that again, he would be fired on the spot. Jake White was off limits, they feel bad for what happened to his daughter, but it was an accident.

Dan argued the facts, but they wanted to hear none of it, he was an untouchable rich kid, that's the way he viewed it. Surprisingly, Dan didn't quit the force, instead he stayed on, eventually becoming Lieutenant. Dan, never forgot his wife and daughter, he visited their graves often. Bringing their favorite flower with him, the Japanese Rose. Dan did make one promise to them both, that no matter what he would set things right.

10

A TIME TO KILL

GRANT WAS BACK AT HIS HOTEL ROOM, CLEANING HIMSELF UP, doctoring his wounds. By the time he was done, he had almost gone through another bottle of bourbon to ease the pain. Maybe being drunk was his best bet to pull off what the killer wanted from him next. He was to kill a man, not just any man though, he was to kill Todd Johnson.

Johnson's real name was Todd Kingsman, aka Crazy King. The man had ties with the mob, to put it mildly, Todd was their muscle. Whenever the mod needed someone to get their hands dirty, Todd was the guy they called. He had a way of making people talk, also ways of keeping them quiet. The man also had a way of making trouble disappear as well. He wasn't a guy to be trusted, or trifled with. When the FBI brought the mob bosses down that he had been working for. Kingsman immediately cut himself a deal.

Todd told the authorities that if they put him in a witness protection program, he would testify against his former employers. The feds jumped on that opportunity and inked out a deal. Kingsman did as he said he would do and he testified at a court hearing. With that information the crime lords were sent to prison for a very long time.

The FBI kept their end of the deal too, sending him to Dover with a new identity.

That is why the maniac that has Mary, wants Todd dead. He was another one of those people deemed not worthy of a second chance in life. And why not make Grant do his dirty work, while he concentrates on more important matters. This was going to be one of the hardest things Dawson had ever thought about doing. Sure the man was a scumbag but it didn't mean that he had the right to take the man's life. Grant strapped his nine millimeter to his lower back and a smaller gun to his ankle. He didn't know what he was going to encounter with a man like that.

Now in the suburbs of Dover, which was the part of town where the people with a title lived. With their nice houses and fancy cars, these were the type of people that could get away with murder in a sense. Somehow Kingsman managed to find himself living amongst them. So this is where the killer was sent to live out the rest of his days, Grant thought.

Never would he have figured that the FBI would go through such lengths for a hitman of the mob. These thoughts spurred Grant on, made him angry, maybe even angry enough to kill, if it meant saving Mary's life. All the houses looked the same to Grant, though the killer assured him he would know Kingsman's house when he laid eyes upon it.

There was one house in the neighborhood that was a different color than the rest of the others. The house stood out like a sore thumb, it was painted blue with a red fence that stretched around the whole of the house. Todd, more than likely did this to get under his fellow neighbors skin. Grant pulled his vehicle up across the street and got out. He scanned the area to see if anyone was out and about, lucky for him the coast was clear.

He casually walked up to the house, like he had been there a thousand times before. Again he looked around to see if there were any eyes on him before letting himself in. He searched the house over, there was no sign of Todd. When Grant went to leave, he took a blow to the back of the head and the room started to spin. He tried to fight it off until he was hit again, that blow knocked him out cold.

Water was thrown in Grant's face, the cold from the liquid woke him up. He tried to stand and he could not, he fought to move but was unable to do so. When his vision cleared, Kingsman was standing in front of him grinning from ear to ear. He looked like a man that was about to have himself some fun, but it wasn't going to be the good kind of fun.

"Who sent you?" Todd asked.

"No one," Grant mumbled.

"Speak up!"

"No one! I'm here of my own free will."

"Really?" Todd grunted. "Is that why you were packing heat?"

"Got to protect yourself." Grant smiled in defiance.

"A wise guy, I like that in most people." He put a hand on Grant's shoulder, "I have a way of dealing with guys like you." Kingsman punched him in the gut three swift times, "Now do you want to talk?"

Grant coughed and laughed, then coughed some more, "Is that all you've got?"

"I'm going to enjoy breaking you." Todd beat the hell out of Grant, by the time he was done, Grant had a cut above his right eye, his left eye was damn near swollen shut. Blood leaked from his nose and mouth and the other cuts on his face. "Alright friend, I'm going to give you one more chance. Who sent you?" Grant spate blood at Todd, refusing to give an inch.

Kingsman laughed as he walked out of the room, and came back with a flat head screwdriver. "You're making this fun for me." He chuckled. Then took the screwdriver and drove it down into Grant's leg, hard enough it almost went out the backside. Instead of crying out in pain, Grant began to laugh which got under Todd's skin even more.

The ex mobster walked out of the room again, this time mumbling curse words under his breath. Grant took this as his chance to try and break free. He rocked the chair he was tied to back and forth until it tipped over, sending him crashing to the floor with enough force that the chair broke into several pieces. He managed to get his hands from behind his back, though his hands were still tied together at the wrists.

Grant got to his feet, pulled the screwdriver out of his leg, and hid out of sight waiting for Todd to return. As soon as the man returned, Grant didn't give him a chance to react. He lunged at the man, stabbing him in the back with the screwdriver. Kingsman was struggling with pulling at the object stuck in his upper back. Which gave Dawson enough time to grab his gun off the counter taking aim at Todd's head. Once Kingsman realized what had happened he began to beg for his life.

Todd held his blood covered hands up in front of him, "Please, don't kill me. I didn't mean anything by what I was doing to you. I was just protecting myself."

Grant hit Todd in the face with the butt of the gun, when he staggered Grant took hold of the screwdriver, pushing it further into the flesh of Todd's back. Kingsman screamed in agony, thinking of ways he was going to kill the man causing him so much pain. His body however crumbled, and he fell to his knees. "Do you like that? Do you enjoy the pain that you're feeling? Not a lot of fun when it's you that's being tortured is it?!"

"This is breaking and entering, and assault with a deadly weapon on top of that," Todd said.

He hit Todd in the face with the gun again, "And what is it that you were trying to do to me?"

"Protecting my home. And boy would I hate to be you when the cops show up."

"Oh?" Grant laughed. "Why is that?"

"Because the government owes me, which means all the pigs in this town has to protect me, whether they like it or not."

Grant's smile widened, "Let me fill you in on a little secret, Kingsman."

"You do know me." Todd snorted.

"I do," he answered. "I know everything about you. It was once my job to keep an eye on scum like you. You kill innocent people for your bosses, hurt others when they've done nothing wrong. All for the sake of selling fear, so your employer can extort money from those same hard-working men and women. Guys like you don't change, and if not for the deal you made. Your sorry ass would be rotting away in some prison cell."

"Get to the point."

"The point is, if I killed you right this instant, while you're on your knees begging for your life. Do you think anyone would care? The FBI doesn't give a damn about you, neither do the local cops, neither do I. Lucky for you that I'm not a killer," Grant explained. He lowered the gun giving Kingsman the opportunity that he had been waiting for. Todd lunged for the weapon, knocking it from Grant's hand. What Todd didn't count on was Grant's strong instinct to live. The last thing Kingsman expected to see was the screwdriver that was stuck in his back, being plunged into his neck.

The blow delivered was deadly, Todd's carotid artery had been torn by the end of the screwdriver. He was holding both of his hands to his neck trying to slow the bleeding. It was of no use, the warm red liquid flowed from between his fingers. Not only that, he could feel the blood gurgling up from his throat into his mouth. Kingsman fell to his knees, a look of shock and disbelief was in his eyes. Seconds later the man known as Crazy King was dead at Grant's feet, "Stupid son of a bitch." He tossed the screwdriver beside the body.

Grant took out his phone and took a picture of Kingsman before walking out of the house. He had a feeling it would be days before anyone would care enough about his whereabouts. Even when they find him dead in his house who will really give a damn. Kingsman had ties to the mob, it was only a matter of time before they had their revenge.

The sky above was becoming cloudy, the wind began to blow, and raindrops pelted the ground. This felt like a bad omen, almost as if something was letting Dawson know that there would be a price to pay later down the road. Though he had every intention of not allowing there to be bloodshed, it happened regardless. He had hoped that Todd might work with him if it meant saving his own hide. That he would play the part of a dead man to appease a bloodthirsty killer.

None of that mattered now, there was no use dwelling on it, what was done was done. Grant was far enough out of the suburbs that he could pull the vehicle over without drawing attention to himself. He took out his phone sending the picture of a dead Kingsman to the murderer. Allowing him or her, or perhaps both, to see that the task at hand had been accomplished. Grant waited for a response back but didn't get one in return. It was later that evening when he received a text, he was sent a street address along with a time frame.

A little after midnight he pulled up to the location given to him, it was a back alley on the lower side of town. Where the homeless drank and slept, and drug dealers sold their goods. Why would the killer sent him to such a place without instruction? He had no idea what he was looking for, or what must be done. This was a lawless part of town, they didn't appreciate new visitors. Though that didn't sway him in the least, he has dealt with plenty of places where the law was hated.

Grant searched the alleys thoroughly, during the search he stumbled upon some gang members that didn't take kindly to his presence. With a little persuasion, he talked them into leaving him alone. Actually he pulled his gun on the three young men and threatened to shoot them. They could see it in his eyes that if either of them tried anything he would kill them. The three guys moved out of Grant's way, allowing him to get by without any trouble.

The search continued, still he had no idea what he was looking for and began feeling like he was sent out on a wild goose chase. If that was the case then the murderer did this as a distraction, so he could plot his next move. As he was getting ready to leave, he heard a noise coming from inside one of the dumpsters to the left of him. Grant approached the dented dumpster with his gun drawn.

"Come out of the dumpster now!" He demanded. No answer, instead another loud thud came from within, "If you don't want to come out of your own free will, then I'm going to drag your ass out."

Again, no reply. He reached his hand out, grasped the lid. With a shaky hand he raised the lid it up.

With the gun tight in his grip, Grant looked over the edge and inside the dumpster. At first, he couldn't see anything except trash and torn trash bags. He puts his gun away, trading it for his flashlight when the light reflected inside, Grant sworn he heard a faint whimper. Immediately, he jumped over and inside the dumpster full of trash. He dug through, shoving the trash to the sides, at times even throwing the trash to the outside. When he got to the bottom is when he found her. Mary was bound and gagged, the look in her eyes said all that he needed to know.

Grant took a knife from his pocket, opened it and began cutting the duct tape that had her wrists and ankles bound. Once Mary was freed she pulled the tape from her mouth then hugged him tight. "Thank god you're alive." Grant let out a sigh of relief as he hugged her back. Feeling her safe and sound in his arms was something he would never forget.

"I didn't think I would be." Mary cried. "They threatened to kill me over and over again."

"Let's get you out of here and to a hospital." He insisted. "After that, you can tell the police what happened."

"No!" Mary belted.

Grant helped a weakened Mary out of the dumpster, he held her close as he helped her down the alley and towards his vehicle. Mary's hair was a mess, her lipstick was smeared, her mascara stained the sides of her face. It must have been hell for her not knowing if she would live or die.

"Why not?" He opened the passenger side door, helping her into the vehicle. "We need to make sure you're not hurt, and the police needs to know what happened to you." He jumped in the vehicle and fired up the engine, shifted the gear into drive and pulled away. Mary stayed silent for most of the drive, eventually she began to speak again.

"Did you call the cops for help after I was taken?" Mary asked.

"I did not."

"Why?"

"We can talk more at your place," Grant responded.

Her body trembled at the thought of going back there. "I can't go back not right now." When she turned to look at Grant, the fear in her eyes was obvious. "Can we go to your hotel room instead?"

"Sure." He smiled faintly. He wasn't about to refuse her request, the lady had been through enough and who was he to add more to it. Mary was a strong-willed woman, even now she put on a strong front. But the cracks in her facade were starting to show, at any moment she could break down and cry. "Is there a reason you don't want to go back to your place?"

"I don't want to be alone."

"You won't be alone, I will stay with you."

Mary took a deep breath, "It's hard to explain, can we just leave it at that."

It was around one in the morning when they had gotten to the hotel. Mary was in the shower cleaning herself up, while Grant was sitting at the table pouring himself a small glass of bourbon. By the time she was done with the shower and fully clothed, he had already drank two glasses and working on his third. Thoughts had stirred in his mind, he was happy to find her alive and well, still things didn't feel right.

Though there was a nagging feeling that something was amiss, the maniac could have easily killed her. Made his life a living hell by sending his mind into a frenzy. Which would have ruined the chances of him solving this case. The murderer had him where he wanted him, pushed him to his limits, tested to see how far Grant was willing to go to save her. The killer could have kept this game going for as long as he or she wished, pushing him to the brink of madness.

For some reason he or she decided to end the game after his run-in with Kingsman. Maybe the fun had been had and boredom set in if that was the case, why spare Mary's life. Or perhaps this was just a distraction to throw Grant off his pursuit, while others could be taken without fear of being caught. Soon he would find the answers he sought after and more.

“Is this how you spend all your nights?” Mary asked, taking a seat at the other end of the table.

“Only when I need to calm my nerves,” Grant said. “Which is every night.” He took another drink of his bourbon. “Would you like a drink?”

“After the week I’ve had do you even have to ask,” she replied stiffly.

Grant reached for one of the plastic cups on the table, turned it upright and poured some bourbon in it before handing the cup over. He watched as she took a swig, her face turned red and she began to cough. “When was the last time you had a drink?” He smirked.

“The day you left.” She lifted the cup to her lips and took another drink. The second went down a lot smoother than the first, “Good stuff.” Her voice was raspy and dry, though that didn’t stop her from taking the third drink.

“It’s the cheap shit.” Grant laughed. “Can’t afford the good stuff.” He kept his eyes on Mary, waiting for her to talk about the events that will change her life forever.

“You’re waiting aren't you?” She asked.

“For what?”

“Come on, Grant. You’re waiting for me to talk.” She downed the bourbon then handed the cup back to him, “Pour me another.” He lifted the bottle, tilted it slightly, the brownish liquid ran from the bottle down into the cup. When done he passed the cup back to her. “Just ask,” Mary blurted out.

“I don’t want to push it.” Grant smiled ever so slightly. “My main concern is how you are feeling?”

“Well,” she paused. “I’m not dead, so that’s a plus. They didn’t hurt me physically, but mentally-” She took a deep breath in, exhaled out. “Mentally, they tried to break me. At least one of them did.”

“You keep saying they. Were there two of them?”

“Yes there were two killers.” She trembled at her own answer, remembering everything that had happened to her over the past few days.

“I hate doing this, but I need to know everything,” Grant said.

"Where do I start?"

"From the beginning." He gave a worrisome smile, that he hoped she didn't pick up on.

She nodded in agreeance, "Before I walked out of the restaurant a lady stopped me." Mary began.

"Miss, can I have a moment of your time?" A female voice called out.

Mary turned to see a lady wearing all black, with a hoodie over her head and sunglasses covered her eyes. The lady looked strange and possibly crazed. Still she felt compelled to speak with her. "Is there a problem? Do I know you from somewhere?" She asked.

"Of course not." The lady smiled. "It's about the man you were sitting with, he can't be trusted."

"Why would you say such things?"

The lady held up her hand to quiet Mary, "Let's not discuss this here, shall we step outside." She pointed to the door, "After you." Mary hesitated for a moment, she was unsure if she could trust the lady enough to follow her out of the restaurant. If something were to transpire inside, at least there would be witnesses, and Grant would be there to protect her as well. Stepping outside would make her vulnerable, though she would do so just to hear what the lady had to say.

"This better be worth my time," Mary said, walking out the door first.

"Oh, it will be," the lady muttered as she followed behind her.

"Now if you don't mind, explain to me now what you couldn't tell me inside." Mary demanded.

"Do you really think you get to make demands little girl." The woman hissed.

"I think that I can walk right back inside and tell that man I'm with all about you," Mary responded with a hateful tone.

The lady smiled brightly, "You won't be getting that chance little girl." Before Mary could speak, a hand reached around from behind her placing some sort of rag on her nose and mouth. It was then she realized that she had been tricked, unfortunately it was too late for her to react now. She was losing consciousness, the more she tried to fight, the more her body was fading. The last thing Mary had seen before passing out was the woman laughing at her.

Mary felt something or someone violently shaking her, they seemed upset that she was still unconscious or perhaps she was dead. It wasn't clear which was the case to her yet, "Wake up bitch!"A voice shouted. Mary felt a sharp pain to the side of her face, "I said wake up damn you!" She was still groggy from whatever drug that was used to knock her out.

Her eyesight was fuzzy, though she could still make out the figure standing before her. The person was slim, a hair taller than herself. And apparently, this person liked to play dress up. As he or she was wearing a black spandex outfit, black shoes, black gloves, along with a wicked looking black and white mask that smiled back at her. "Now the real fun can begin." Mary recognized the voice right off, it was the female from the restaurant.

The oddly dressed lady went to hit her again when another voice called out from the darkness, "Don't be so rude to our new guests, Hera." She lowered her hand and stepped to the side, "That's better." Another figure walked closer, Mary could see that this person was dressed up as well. This figure wore a black robe with a hood that covered the whole of the face, except for the glowing red eyes staring down at her. "You're not allowed to hurt her, Hera." The figure scolded. Unlike the female, this person used a voice distorter.

"Sorry Hades." She whimpered. "I was just having some fun."

"Take your fun elsewhere." Hades demanded. The female with the name Hera lowered her head and walked away like she had just committed a sin. "You have to forgive her, she's very impulsive. Hera lacks the self-control that I have."

"Why have you done this to me?" Mary mumbled, barely able to make sense of her own question.

"Speak up child. I cannot hear you," Hades replied.

"Why are you doing this to me?!" She shouted.

"Because we were left with no choice," the figure responded back.

"What do you mean by that?"

"The man you were with, we asked him to leave, to forget about the murders and get out town immediately. If he refused then the people he cared for would get hurt, he refused."

"And you're going to use me to send a message?" Mary interjected.

"In a way," the figure replied.

"In a way?" She snarled. "What does that even mean?"

"We're going to use you to test his metal, see how far he will go to save your life," Hades replied.

"What if he doesn't go along with your plan? Will you kill me like you did the others?"

The figure that stood before her started laughing, "Killing you does not fit into my plans. I only kill the ones that deserve it, whether your man fails or not will not decide your fate."

"Then let me go!" She pleaded with him to no avail.

"All in due time," Hades said. "It is late and you need to rest, we will have more time to talk later on." The figure knelt down and shackled her leg, then he took the restraints from her wrists. "There is a bed in the corner, Hera will be here in the morning to feed you. If you try to escape, you will die." The dark figure turned and walked away.

Mary waited for the person to be out of sight, she ignored the warning he had given her. She tugged at the chain that was shackled to her ankle, there was no give whatsoever. She traced the chain towards the wall and gave it another hard tug. It did no good, she was stuck there, she couldn't escape that night. Mary decided she would do as she was told until the opportunity presented itself for her to make a run for it. She laid down on the bed in the corner of the room with only the dim light to keep her company.

The next day, bright and early that morning, Hera came in with food as promised. The lady was still dressed in black but had a different mask on that leered back at her. The lady wasn't too happy with the fact that she had to be responsible for the prisoner. And it showed in the tone of her voice and her body movements. "Time to eat, bitch." She kicked the side of the bed. When that didn't work

Hera grabbed Mary's hair and pulled her out of the bed and onto the floor.

"What the hell!" Mary shouted out of instinct, not realizing that could set the crazed lady off at a moments notice.

"Get your ass in the chair it's time to eat!" She demanded. Mary slowly got to her feet, she went to sit down but before she could, Hera shoved her down onto the chair. She then shoved the tray of food into Mary's lap demanding that she eats, and do so quickly or go without.

When she went to eat, though Hera wasn't done with her yet. "Did you think about that first bite?" She asked her. "I could have easily poisoned you, or perhaps Hades did so for me." Mary dropped the spoon from her hand, it landed in the eggs on her plate with a splat. She had a look of panic in her eyes which seemed to please Hera, "Eat or I will enjoy shoving that garbage down your throat."

"Why do you torture me? Didn't your boss say to play nice?" She picked up the spoon using it to take another bite of eggs.

That comment sent Hera over the edge, she took the tray away from her and threw it across the room. "Go without!" She hissed then stormed out of the room. Mary was lucky that was all that transpired, things could have gone a lot differently if Hera was acting on her own. Though something told her that the one that calls himself Hades is the brains of the outfit, while Hera was just a pawn in his sick and twisted game.

Hours had passed and she was becoming hungry, so much so that she was feeling queasy. She even thought about going over to where the tray lay on the floor and eat the eggs off the floor itself. Mary had an iron deficiency, which meant if she didn't eat at certain times she would become ill, possibly even pass out. The thought came and went, she refused to degrade herself further for the amusement of her tormentors.

"You don't look so good," Hades said, walking out of the darkness, he was wearing the same exact costume as last time.

"I have an iron deficiency," Mary said, fighting against the urge to fall over in front of her captor.

"I didn't know that."

"How could you?" She responded back. "You don't know anything about me."

"Wise assumption. Allow me to get you something more to eat, I will return shortly." Thirty more minutes passed before he was back with something more for her to eat. "I know this isn't much, but it's better than nothing." Hades handed her over a ham sandwich along with a small bag of chips. As she ate he pulled up another chair and took a seat. Even though Mary couldn't see his eyes, she could feel his ice-cold stare gazing at her, studying her.

"Something wrong?" She asked.

"What you said earlier." Hades began. "About us not knowing each other-"

"And?" Mary interrupted. "You trying to say that you want to get to know me?

"Is that such a bad thing?"

"You did kidnapped me, drugged me, on top of that you chained me to a wall." She finished her sandwich, took a drink of water and finished her sentence, "Plus, killers usually don't want to open up to their victims."

"Would you believe me if I said that I wasn't a killer?" Hades responded.

"You murder innocent people." She spate. "How is that not being a killer?"

He held his gaze on her for a minute or two longer, the red eyes glowing as he did so. "That is what I was afraid of, you have passed judgment down upon me already. How can I explain myself to you, if you are not willing to open your mind."

"Then explain it to me, Hades," Mary sarcastically replied. "But before you do. Tell me, why are the two of you using greek god names as aliases?"

"Greek gods are a symbol of power and respect. They also decide one's fate as do we."

"Then why not call yourself Zeus instead of Hades?" Mary found herself curious about the answer he would give.

"Hades chose who would live and who would die. Who deserved

a second chance and who would be taking a trip to the underworld. Zeus did not concern himself with such things, therefore his name was not fitting of me."

"Both men pursued power, is that what you seek as well?"

"I only seek the power to do what is just," Hades answered. "Nothing more, nothing less."

Mary wanted to argue the point with this madman, but if she did the conversation would end. And she wanted to see how much information this person was willing to give up. If she was lucky enough to live, then the information would be useful to the police and Grant. "Let's forget about that for the time being. I want to know something and I don't mean to be to forward."

"Go on," Hades said.

Mary cleared her throat, she was somewhat afraid of the killer figuring out her true intentions, "Are you a male or female? I mean I can tell that your companion is a female. But with the way you dress, it's hard to tell."

"Why do you ask?"

She thought hard about her response, "Well, if you want me to trust what you have to say then I need to know."

"Hmm." Hades seemed a little apprehensive about answering the question. "If you must know, I am a male. That is the truth, no harm in telling you since you already know Hera is a female. Does that answer your question, Miss-"

"Maddison, Mary Maddison. Is this what you do with all your victims?"

"Again, Miss Maddison. You're a guest, not a victim," he responded. "You have nothing to worry about."

"Tell that to, Hera." Marry muttered.

"She will not harm you without my consent." Hades reassured her.

"What do you have on her? Or is she just crazy like you?"

"We're not crazy, but we will get to that. As far as Hera goes, she follows me of her own free will."

"Why?" She persisted further.

"She was once seen as one of the unclean." Just when he was about to continue, he was interrupted by Hera. She came in wearing the same clothing the night they kidnapped her. She bowed to him, then whispered something in his ear, turned back around and walked away. "It appears that I have some business to attend to. Just when this conversation was getting good. We'll speak again soon until then enjoy your stay, and remember don't try to escape." Hades stood from his chair and proceeded to walk away.

That night Mary was awoken by cynical laughter followed by screams of anguish and pain. The thought of another poor soul being tortured close by was too much for her to handle. She curled up into a fetal position on the bed and tried to tune out the noise. The next morning came slower than usual, just like last time Hera walked in with food. More mind games ensued, though this time Mary kept to herself, taking the mental abuse. Afraid that if she mouthed back she would be next to suffer.

A couple of days had passed, and Mary began to wonder if her captors would ever let her go. Hades walked in and answered that question before she would get the chance to ask. "This is going to be the last few hours we spend together, Miss Madison. Before we say our goodbyes, I owe you answers. I chose Hera as a mistake made by God that needed to be rectified. For some reason I couldn't bring myself to end her life, it was as if I could see something different in her. Unlike god, I gave her a true second chance. By her own choice she has been with me since."

Mary was happy to learn that she would be released, still she wanted more information. "What makes a person unclean?" She asked.

"God gives a human the second chance, no matter how undeserving they are of it. The law turns a blind eye towards a crime that a man or woman commits, no matter how bad it truly is. If that said person has an important last name, or if they have lots of money, kids are no different. These are the ones deemed unclean."

"And you fix it by killing them?" She could barely keep her anger at bay.

"I merely take away what God gave to them. Afterward, I let the world see the mistakes made by God and man."

"What about your first victim, what did he ever do to you?" She hissed. "He was just a child coming into his own, with a bright future ahead of him."

Hades laughed, "He's the one that started all of this." He had a rag in one hand and a bottle in the other, he doused the rag tossing the now empty bottle to the side. "This conversation has run its course." He pressed the rag to her face, not a second later she was out. When Mary woke up, she was in complete darkness. Her hands were tied behind her back, her ankles were bound together.

"After that I found you tied up in the dumpster." Grant finished the sentence for her.

She nodded, "And here we are."

"They didn't hurt you in any way?" He asked.

"No, the one that called herself Hera was unpleasant enough. Hades, refused to let her harm me, guess I was lucky for that."

"That's a relief." Grant smiled, taking another drink of bourbon. "Can I ask you something, it might not be too pleasant."

"I can handle it," she said.

"Did it feel like you were being watched? Even at your place?" He questioned.

"Come to think of it, I felt like that for days before the kidnapping happened." Mary shivered just thinking about it. "Why?"

"These killers are smart," Grant said. "They stalk their victims, get to know everything about them. Their habits, where they eat, where they go shopping. When they feel the time is right, the victims are usually taken from inside their homes in the middle of the night."

"At midnight." Her shaky hands lifted the glass of bourbon to her lips, finishing the tiny bit left in the bottom.

"But they didn't do that with you," he said. "On top of that, they let you live. Wonder why?"

"Hades said this had to do with you not leaving town," Mary replied. "The plan was not to hurt me, but to push you to your limits. See how far you would have been willing to go to save my life."

"Makes sense." Grant sighed, "If I had left, none of this madness would have transpired."

"This isn't your fault, Grant. They're afraid of you that's why they wanted you out of town. You did the right thing by staying."

"If only it were that simple." He went to pour himself another glass of bourbon but the bottle was empty. "Damn." Grant threw the bottle across the room, shattering it against the wall on impact.

Mary jumped, looking over at him startled, "Was that really necessary?" She asked, her eyes meeting his.

"No, but it made me feel better," he responded. He should have thought more on what he was doing, it was stupid of him to act the way he had. Doing something as foolish as what he had done, could get him kicked out of the hotel. Possibly getting law enforcement called, which was one thing he needed to avoid.

"Then why are you acting a damn fool." She scolded him.

"You're right, Mary. I lost control there for a minute, it can't happen again." Grant went to stand, but the pain shooting through his body made him sit back down.

"Something wrong?" She glared over at him, not realizing the pain that he was in at that moment in time.

"It's nothing." He looked down at his hand, it was covered with his blood, the wounds had opened up again. "Is there more to the story?" He winced in pain again this time feeling faint.

Mary took a hard look at Grant, his demeanor had changed, his face was pale, beads of sweat forming on his forehead. She leaned over the table, seen that his hand and shirt was covered in blood. "Oh my god!" She exclaimed. "You're hurt!"

"It's none of your concern," he replied coldly.

Mary stood from her chair, she was done taking his bullshit but she couldn't very well let him die. She believed that he was the only one capable of stopping the killers. "Take off your shirt and let me see, or I rip it off your sorry ass."

"Have it your way, you won't like what you see." His legs were too weak for him to stand, so he stayed seated to remove his shirt.

She couldn't believe her eyes, Grant had cuts and gashes from his stomach to his arms, some bleeding a little, some seeping blood. The worst of the wounds was the one closest to his pelvis. It stretched the length of his hand. The wound looked like it had been doctored up once but must have reopened. "My god, Grant. What did they do to you?"

"Simple, I was put through the ringer." He chuckled but the pain made it hard for him to laugh.

"This is no time for jokes, you could bleed to death. Do you have a first aid kit at least?" Her hands were on her hips and she was shooting daggers in his direction.

"In the bathroom, under the sink."

She motioned to the bed, "Go lay down, I will doctor your wounds." It was clear that she wasn't going to take no for an answer. Grant used all the strength he had left in his body to stand and stagger his way towards the bed. He hovered momentarily then fell into bed, back first. Mary walked back into the room with the first aid kit in her hands. She sat on the bed next to him, digging through the kit. She laid out a few gauze pads, a bottle of rubbing alcohol, and some bandages.

He watched her put aside the things she needed, building up the nerve to say what he felt in the moment. "I'm sorry." Seemed to be the only words that would come to him.

"For what?" She asked, concentrating on the task at hand. She doused the wash rag she had gotten from the bathroom with rubbing alcohol. "This might hurt." Mary used the rag to clean the wounds on his chest and the large gash across his stomach. Grant winced in pain, almost cried out when she began to clean the largest wound. This brought a small smile to Mary's face, along with a small amount of pleasure.

While she was applying the salve, Grant found his words again. "What I am trying to say is that I am sorry for what I said in the restaurant that night. I would say that I didn't mean to hurt you, but that wouldn't be the truth."

She was tapping the gauze pads to his wounds, then paused to look up at him. "So you meant to hurt me?"

"Somewhat."

"Are you telling me this to make yourself feel better?"

"I want you to understand why I said what I did."

She went back to finishing up tapping the gauze pads to his wounds, "I think I understand," Mary said. "You wanted to protect me. And after what I've been through, I realize others will use me to get to you. You did what you felt was right. Raise up, I have to put the bandages on your stomach and back."

He raised himself upright, allowing her to wrap the ace bandages around his chest, stomach and back. "That and-" Grant caught himself mid-sentence.

"And, what?" Mary asked.

"I purposely tried to push you away for my sake. All of these unexpected feelings came flooding back, it scared me."

"You hurt me, Grant. I poured my heart out to you, begged you to give us another chance. And you shoved it back into my face, I get that you wanted to protect me. Hell, I even understand that you wanted to protect yourself from your own feelings."

"Mary, I-" Grant tried to cut her off and explain himself further, but she was having none of it.

"I'm not done yet!" Mary hissed. Her anger towards him was coming back in waves, "You made me feel so small that night like I didn't mean a damn thing to you. I hate you right now, but for some stupid reason, I still love you. With all these different emotions running through me, love, hate, fear, I can still see the truth. I just need to hear it from you." Mary finished wrapping Grant's wounds and sat there staring at him, waiting for him to say something.

"I-" He was hesitant to speak. "Truth is, I am still in love with you. Those types of feelings get to me because I haven't felt anything like love in a long time. Caring about others hasn't been one of my strong points, that's what makes it easier for me to take down the bad guys. There's nothing they can do to get to me, to make me weak. I tried to put my feelings for you to the side, as you can see that didn't go over so well."

The phone in the room started ringing, Grant and Mary looked at each other with surprise. He was taken back the most, this was the first time the hotel phone had rung in the weeks he's been staying there. Grant reached over and picked up the phone, "Hello?"

On the other end of the line was Lieutenant Harris, "Thank god you're alive."

"Why are you calling my room instead of my cell phone?"

"I've been trying to call your cell phone," Harris replied. "Thanks for the heads up that you were still among the living."

"Battery must be dead." He ignored the words of concern like always, "Is there something you need?"

"We have another dead body on our hands." Harris grunted.

"Who?" Already knowing the answer to that question.

"Todd Johnson, looks like a home invasion gone wrong."

"We both know he had ties to the mob," Grant said. "Maybe those ex-bosses of his finally got some payback."

"Could be true. He was scum anyways. My main concern about calling is, Mary. She hasn't been working lately, getting worried. Know anything about that?"

Grant looked over at Mary, a sign that the conversation was about her. She shook her head, letting him know not to say a word of the things that had transpired over the weeks. "Don't worry about, Mary. She's been with me, we've been catching up on old times."

"I see." The tone of his voice said that he didn't believe his story. "Since that situation is cleared up. How are you holding up? Last time we meet you didn't look so good."

"Had a rough couple of days, but things have gotten better since. I have to go, Harris. Call me if anything else happens." He hung up the phone with haste, not giving Harris a chance to question him further. "You know that we have to tell him the truth sooner or later." He said while looking over at her.

"I know," Mary said. "I hate lying to, Harris. He's been so nice to me, almost like a second dad."

"A lot has changed since I've been gone," Grant said. "Tell him soon. Alright?"

"Alright," she said. "I'm getting tired, think I'm ready for some sleep."

"Agreed, it's been a long few days." Grant yawned. "I'll sleep on the couch, lucky for me I got the bigger room. You can take the bed."

Mary laid down on the bed and patted the mattress, "Sleep beside me, I don't want to be alone." He smiled in return and laid back down on the bed beside her. He brushed the hair out of her face, then leaned over and kissed her forehead. She gave a faint smile, rolled over and closed her eyes, letting sleep take her.

Grant stayed awake a while longer, thinking about the things he was forced to do to ensure Mary's safe return. He went through hell and back, walked the lines of insanity, pushed his body to the limits. What scared him the most out of all it was the fear of losing another loved one. This time he got lucky and Mary's life was spared. He felt as though he had to do something to solve this case soon and get his ass out of town for good. Tomorrow is a new day, and it was time for him to get the job done.

11

FRIEND FROM THE PAST

THE NEXT MORNING CAME QUICKER THAN MARY THOUGHT IT WOULD, rays of light shined down on her face through the hotel window, waking her from slumber. She turned over to her right, expecting Grant to still be beside her. She wasn't too surprised when her hand felt nothing more than the empty sheets of the bed. She opened her eyes and saw a note left on the pillow next to her. Mary reached for the folded up paper without giving it a second thought she unfolded the note. Fear raced through her like a runaway train, this was not a note from Grant, but from her captors.

Grant woke up at around six o'clock that morning, not wanting to wake Mary he eased his way out of the bed. He skipped his morning routine, except for throwing on some clean clothes before rushing out the door. There was no time for shaving or showering that morning. He had one thing on his mind, going down to the precinct and have a word with, Lieutenant Harris. What he didn't expect to find when he got to the precinct was pure and utter chaos.

His friend was standing in the front lobby giving out orders to the other officers. Some seemed distracted, while others looked lost and panicky. All while the Lieutenant demanded those officers to get their heads out of their asses or hit the bricks.

Grant approached Harris with a look of bewilderment, “What in the hell is going on around here?” He asked.

“Same shit different day.” Dan grumbled. “Tell you the truth, I’m not sure what to think about these days.”

“Haven’t seen the precinct worked up like this in a long time.”

“What the fuck would you know?” Harris’s voice was loud and mean. “You haven’t been around for years to know what goes on here.”

Dawson held up his hands in defense, “Not here to cause a scene. Just needing to have a word, I understand if that’s asking too much right now.”

“Damn, do you always have to put me in these tight spots. Follow me to my office.”

Grant was somewhat perplexed when Harris lead him into Captain Simons office. “Won’t Simons have our heads for being in here?” He asked.

The Lieutenant blatantly ignored what Grant had to say about being in the Captain’s office. “Have a seat.” He motioned to the chair on the other side of the desk.

“I prefer to stand.” Grant smirked. It was a nervous smirk nonetheless, he didn’t want to run the risk of being thrown in jail. Or worse, being tossed out of town.

Dan pointed at the chair a second time, “If you want to talk then have a seat. Nothing’s going to happen, trust me.”

He did as Harris asked, “Still not sure why we're here instead of your office.”

“Well my friend, you’re looking at the new Captain of precinct twelve,” he answered with a smile that stretched from ear to ear.

“How is that even possible? Simons would rather die than give up her position on the force.”

“What, no congratulations?” Dan laughed. “I thought you would be happy to see me sitting behind this desk. You always said I deserved it more than her.”

“I am happy for you, just confused is all.” None of this made a bit of sense. He couldn’t make heads or tails of what was going on.

"Tell you the truth, so am I," Harris said. "The only reason I am sitting here now is that Simon's disappeared about two weeks ago. Not a soul has heard from her, or seen her since."

About the same time Mary was taken against her will, Grant thought to himself, "What have you done to try and find her?"

"Everything we can do. Searched the streets, her house, talked with family members, nothing has turned up any leads."

Grant ran his fingers nervously through his hair, "Is it possible the killer had something to do with her disappearance?"

"Can't rule that fact out. Isn't there something you need to talk to me about?"

"What about, Simon's?" Grant questioned.

"What about her?" Harris snarled. "Besides, this is the precincts concern not yours. You were brought in to help with the midnight killers case nothing more." His voice sounded angrier than usual. "So talk or leave, I have important matters to attend to."

"Have it your way." Grant shrugged. "I wanted to pass some information along to you."

"This had better be good." The new Captain warned.

Dawson gave a crooked smile, "I've been informed that there are two killers not just one."

Dan's eyes narrowed, "Are you sure?"

"I'm sure," he answered.

"What do you want me to do about it?" The Captain asked.

"I was hoping you would look into it for me."

"Who shared this information with you?" Harris questioned further.

"That person wishes to remain anonymous."

"If you can't tell me who told you, then I'm afraid my hands are tied."

Grant slammed his hands on top of the desk, "It's your job to follow up leads!" He shouted.

"My job is to do what I believe is right!" Harris fired back. "And finding Simon's is the number one priority!"

Grant stood from his chair, "I'm not saying Simon's isn't important. But we have to stop the killers before they hurt someone else. You of all people know this!"

Harris glared at him, his eyes were stone cold sober, "Your time is up. And I'm only going to tell you this once. Don't show your face around here again. If you do, I will have you thrown in jail." This wasn't the same man that Grant remembered from his past. Dan was a man that Grant looked up to for his beliefs. Clearly that wasn't the case any longer, this man before him was bitter and acted as though he hated the world.

"What happened to you?"

"I woke up. You can show yourself out."

"You're a sad man," Grant said, then turned and walked out of the room.

After he left the room, Harris picked up the phone and punched in a number. "This is Harris, do you have everything in order? Good, see you soon," He said before hanging up the phone.

Grant was on his way out of the police precinct when he felt a hand grasp his shoulder. He spun around with his fist pulled back, "Hey wait, it's me Turner." Officer Turner was standing there with his hands up protecting his face.

"Damn it, Turner. Don't sneak up on me like that." Grant hissed. "What is it that you need?"

"I need to have a word with you," Turner responded. He could tell that Grant wasn't in the mood for small talk, "It will only take a minute, I promise."

"You have one minute of my time, that's it."

The officer gave a half-hearted grin, "Follow me to my squad car."

"Why?"

"Don't want any unwanted ears listening in on what I tell you. Could cause trouble if the wrong person heard."

Grant nodded, "Smart man." He motioned for Turner to walk on ahead, "After you."

"Still don't trust me?"

"I don't trust anyone right now."

Turner walked on ahead, glancing back every so often to see if

Grant was still following. He reached into his pants pocket, removed his keys, pressing the unlock button on his remote. The patrol car honked twice, as the doors unlocked. The officer walked around to the driver side door and got inside the vehicle. He pushed a button that rolled down the passenger side window, "You going to get in?"

Grant looked inside the vehicle then back at Turner, "Standing here works for me," he said.

Turner laughed, "I'm not going to hurt you or try and arrest you."

"I like my chances outside of the patrol car." Grant smiled.

"Have it your way, Dawson."

"Okay Turner, enough of the small talk. If you have something important to say, then get on with it."

"Moody as usual," Turner jokingly said. "In all seriousness though, you need to watch your back with the new Captain."

Grant's brow furrowed, his lips turned into a snarl, "Why in the hell would you say that? Harris is like a father to me and you. Hell to most of the precinct!"

"Do you think I like this?" Turner fired back. "Harris has done more for me over the past few years than my own family."

Grant's grip on the door tightened, "If that's true, then why say shit like that?"

"He's been acting weird lately. When I come to him with new leads on the midnight killer case he blows me off. Claims he doesn't have time to chase bogus leads. I tried to push the subject further, and he gets angry quickly. That lead me to go above his head and work with, Captain Simons. Then you came strolling into town on behalf of the Mayor and that really pissed him off."

"Dan is a stubborn man, he doesn't like others stumbling in on his cases. He's been like since I can remember, Harris is a one-man show." Grant defended Harris like he would any family member.

"I am just going to come out with it," Turner said. "I believe Harris is hiding something. Maybe even protecting someone, and I think Simons believed the same."

"Do you have proof of these accusations?"

"Not entirely. The night Simons disappeared I overheard her arguing with the Lieutenant."

"From what I understand that happens quite a bit," Grant said.

"True, but this time was different." Turner insisted.

"How so?"

"The argument seemed more intense than usual," Turner replied. "More violent, like Simons had something on him but he refused to give her straight answers."

"Did you hear what it was about?" Grant asked.

"Can't say that I did."

"Then you're going on pure speculation."

"Just watch your back. Harris isn't acting like himself and you know it. You're just afraid to admit that he could be involved somehow."

"Have a nice day officer." Grant could hear Turner speed off in the patrol car. He wasn't afraid of finding out the truth about his old friend and mentor. Right now, he didn't trust a damn person, not Harris, sure as hell not Turner. He felt guilty that he couldn't even trust Mary, for all he knew the killer could have poisoned her mind.

As much as he wanted to protect her, he still didn't trust her. And yes, Turner was right about how Harris had been reacting lately. How he didn't show much emotion towards the latest victim, the dropping of the keys at the morgue. Most damning of all, was how quick he was to shut Grant down after being told about there being two murders instead of one.

Was that enough to raise suspicions towards the man? It was, but Grant wanted to dig further on his own before pointing fingers. Besides, Harris is a pillar of the community. There would have to be hard evidence brought against him if he were to be guilty. Grant opened the driver side door of his vehicle and climbed inside. Instinct told him to check his cell phone before driving away, seeing how he had it on vibrate for the past few hours. He was right to do so, he had six missed calls from Mary.

The vehicle skidded up to the hotel parking lot. Grant got out of the vehicle and rushed inside the hotel. He ran past the clerk and up the steps to the second floor. He stood outside of his room with his gun drawn, he knocked on the door. At first there was no answer, though shuffling could be heard on the other side. He knocked again, "Mary, it's me Grant. Open the door!" He shouted. Grant was getting ready to kick the door in until it opened slowly. "Mary!" He called out, entering the room cautiously with his gun still in hand.

Grant turned in the nick of time to barely duck a baseball bat aimed at his head. Mary took another swing hitting Grant's arm before she realized it was him, "Sorry, I thought the killers had returned." She frowned. "Are you hurt?"

"No more than usual." Grant smiled, shaking the numbness from his arm. "What's going on? The missed calls, coming back to a baseball bat being swung at me."

"I thought you were the killers," Mary said with tears in her eyes.

Grant pulled Mary into a hug, "You don't have to worry, those maniacs don't know where I stay. You're safe here."

Mary pushed away from him, "You're wrong, Grant. It's not safe here." She took his hand in hers, placing the note from earlier in his hand.

"What's this?"

"Read it and find out for yourself."

He read the note, "Hello, Mary." Was all that was written. Grant didn't question Mary further, instead he wanted to get her out of town and somewhere safe. "Get all your stuff together, I'm getting you out of here," he told her.

"Where will we go?"

"I'm taking you to a friend of mine."

Mary had one small bag in her hand, "Can you take me by the house, I need a few more things."

"Sorry, until this case is solved, you can't go back home."

"But-" Mary started.

"You can't go home. They know where you live, it could be dangerous to go back right now." His words were stern but direct.

"The killers knew that I was here," Mary said. "How do you know for sure they won't find me again."

A thought came to Grant's mind. How did the killers know that she was staying with him? Were they following them? If so, how did he not notice, he always paid attention to his surroundings. Then another thought occurred to him. The sim cards, it's very possible the two used those to hack his phone.

That would mean they had been tracking him the whole time, even listening in on his calls. He didn't give them enough credit at first, thinking it was just one killer feeding his ego. Finding out there were two, and their smart to boot, plus they have a well drawn out plan. Grant realized he made a near fatal mistake by underestimating who he was up against.

"Hand me your phone." He insisted.

"Why?" Mary looked perplexed.

"I think they've been tracking us from our phones."

She handed her phone over to Grant, "What are you going to do?" She asked.

He pitched both their phones on the bed, "Leaving the phones here," he answered.

"Is that safe?" She questioned. "Housekeeping could steal them, then what?"

"As long as we don't have those phones, I don't care what happens to them. Let's get out of here."

Grant and Mary calmly made their way down the hall and towards the steps. Again the clerk paid no mind to who came in or out of the hotel. He helped her into the vehicle, then got in himself and drove away. Halfway out of town Mary decided she wanted some information. "Where are you taking me?" She questioned. Grant didn't answer, instead he was looking in the rearview mirror. "Grant?"

He glanced over at her, "Did you say something?" He asked.

"Never mind." She watched Grant's reactions, he was still looking in the rearview mirror. She also noticed that he was making the vehicle go faster in moderation. "Is something wrong?"

"We're being followed."

"By who?"

"We both know the answer to that question," Grant said.

"Why would they be following us?" Mary said.

"Probably keeping tabs on us. Or perhaps one of them is keeping us occupied."

"What are you going to do?"

Grant reached over pulling her seatbelt tight, "Hang on." He pushed the gas pedal to the floor, sending the vehicle flying down the highway. The car following behind them did the same, whoever it was seemed determined not to let them get away. Both vehicles weaved in and out of traffic topping speeds at over a hundred miles an hour. Grant turned the wheel to make a hard right, the back end of the vehicle swerved, the tires skidded. Somehow he managed to pull off the turn without incident. To his dismay, so did the mysterious driver in pursuit.

"Damn it." He had a crazed look in his eyes when he glanced over at her. "Brace yourself, things are going to get ugly." Grant warned her.

"I don't like that look on your face." Mary shivered. She didn't have to ask what he was about to do, because she already knew the answer. She grabbed onto whatever she could and braced for what was to come.

Without the slightest hesitation, Grant slammed his foot on the brake pedal, causing the vehicle to come to an abrupt stop. The car in pursuit slammed into them with such force that Mary's head almost hit the windshield. His head hit the steering wheel, splitting his forehead wide open. Grant fell out of the driver side of his vehicle. He managed to get back to his feet drawing his gun, he staggered over to the car that was following them. The back end of Grant's vehicle was smashed in, and the tires were up off the ground.

Though the pursuers car was a complete and total wreck, the person driving the car had fled. He hurried back over and helped Mary out of the SUV, "Can you walk?" He asked.

"I think so," Mary replied. "What now?"

"We find another form of transportation, and quickly before the cops get here." He spied a little red beater car parked off in the alleyway. “That car over there will do.” Grant pointed. He ushered her over to a nasty looking red car.

“Out of all the cars to steal, you choose this piece of shit.” Mary said.

“Less conspicuous.” Grant assured her. “I doubt the owner will even care if it’s gone.” He looked around to make sure there were no unexpected eyes watching. He used the butt of his gun to shatter the driver side windshield. Mary on the other hand pulled the passenger side door handle and smiled as it swung open.

“Never hurts to check the door before you bash in the windshield.” Mary smirked before jumping into the car. “Great, it smells like puke in here.” She grumbled.

Grant was laughing when he got inside the car, though she was right about how it smelt. The keys were left in the ignition, just waiting for someone to steal the little red shitty car. He turned the keys a couple of times before the car backfired and started up. “Purrs like a kitten,” he said.

“Sounds like a cat coughing up a hairball,” Mary said. “Will this thing even make it to where you’re taking me?”

“One way to find out.” Grant pulled the gear into drive and the car sputtered down the alleyway.

Later that night Grant and Mary still sputtered down the highway in that shitty red car. But it was to be expected, the car ran hot most of the time forcing them to pull over for thirty minutes at least every two hours. And on top of that, the beater car couldn’t run any faster than fifty miles an hour. Mary had her seat back sleeping. Grant had his eyes on the road, keeping them peeled for anything that could jump out of the darkness.

He began to think about his next move, he knew that he had to keep an eye on Harris, that was a given. Grant refused to accept the fact that he could be apart of the killings, or that he was protecting someone that was.

Still yet, his old friend was acting out of character. Plus the information he had gotten from Turner was rather concerning. But he had thought out a plan of action. First get Mary somewhere safe. Two, find out the identity of the lady that goes by, Hera. Which in turn will lead him straight to the man known as the midnight killer or Hades?

Grant made a left-hand turn that took them off the highway and down a dark narrow road. About that time Mary had woken up, "Where are we?" She asked, groggily looking out the window.

"Getting there," Grant answered. The paved road soon turned to gravel with trees surrounding them on both sides.

"This looks like something out of a scary movie," Mary said.

"Relax, these are good people that I am taking you to stay with." At the end of the road stood an old log cabin, the porch light was on. Other than that it didn't look like anyone was home.

"Are you sure about this?" She asked.

He put the car in park and turned off the engine, "Trust me, you will be safe here." Grant opened the car door and exited the vehicle, he walked over to the passenger side helping Mary out of the car. "Let's go see if anyone is home." Both of them made their way up towards the cabin and up the steps. A clicking noise came from behind them, it reminded him of a pump action shotgun.

"Don't move another inch." A husky voice warned. "Turn around slowly." A tall thin dark-skinned man stood there with a shotgun aimed at their heads. "Well I'll be damned. Is that you, Dawson?"

"In the flesh." Grant smiled. "Mind putting that gun away."

The man lowered the gun, "How long has it been since we last talked?"

"Few years." Grant shrugged, then extended his hand.

The man grabbed Grant's hand with a firm grip, "Good to see you well." He glanced over at, Mary. "Who's the lady?"

"My name is Mary," she said. "And yours?"

"Jones," he replied. "Isaiah Jones."

"Nice to meet you, Isaiah." She gave a faint smile.

"How did you get mixed up with this fool?" Isaiah laughed.

The door to the cabin opened, "Isaiah, is that you out there making all that ruckus?"

"Talking to some friends of mine dear," Isaiah responded back. "That's my wife Tonya."

"Don't be rude," Tonya said. "Invite them inside."

"You heard the lady." Isaiah chuckled. He walked on inside the cabin and waved the others to follow him on inside. The only light was from a fire going in the fireplace. "Sorry about the dimly lit room, we don't like having a lot of lights on in the house. Tonya, will you be a dear and turn the kitchen light on?"

"Yes honey," she replied. Tonya walked into the kitchen and turned the light on, "I will put some tea on for our guests too."

Isaiah ushered them towards the kitchen and offered them a seat at the table, "While my wife is making us some tea, let's talk. Not that I'm not glad to see an old friend. But I know you're not here for a friendly talk." He eyed Grant waiting for the truth to be spilled.

"Truth is, Isaiah. I need a safe place to stay for a friend of mine."

"Is this young lady the friend you are referring to?" Isaiah looked at Mary with a smile on his face.

"Very perceptive of you." Grant's facial expression changed telling a darker tale, Isaiah wasn't even sure he wanted to hear what the man had to say next. "I was brought in to help solve a murder case. Things went south and I got her caught up in this mess. She needs a safe place to stay until I solve this case."

"What about the cops?" Isaiah asked.

"They're on a need to know basis," Grant responded. "Can she stay?"

"Well let's ask her how she feels about staying here," Isaiah said. "Ma'am-"

"Mary." She interrupted.

"Excuse me?"

"Please call me by my name." She finished. "And no, I don't want to stay here. But if I don't then Grant will only worry about me, which will cause more trouble in the long run. And I don't want that either."

Isaiah looked over at Grant before his gaze shifted back to her. "You can stay here if you like. We have a room upstairs, it's yours if you want it."

Mary stared at Grant and smiled, he had been through so much just for her sake. He was already sleep deprived, the bags under his eyes gave that away, stubble grew from his chin. Grant wasn't the man that stared back at her, but another. It was a man concerned for her safety, but willing to do whatever it took to see her stay here, to get her out of his way.

This man had been pushed to his limits and it wouldn't be a good idea to push any further. Though she felt deeply sorry for him, that wasn't the reason she decided to stay. There was this wild look in his eyes that she had never seen before. That look he gave was what made her decision for her.

"Thank you, Isaiah. I believe I will take you up on that offer," Mary said.

About that time, Tonya walked over with a cup of tea for her husband and her guests. She later joined them at the table, whispering something in husband's ear. "Tonya was curious if you wanted to stay as well Grant," Isaiah said.

"No, that wouldn't be wise," he responded. "I need one more favor from you before I leave."

"Name it," Isaiah said.

"I need one of your specialty phones."

"Not a cheap request." Tonya interrupted. She blew the steam from her cup and took a drink of tea. "Though I think we make an exception." She glanced over at Isaiah, "Right dear?"

"Right." Isaiah smiled in return. He wouldn't have refused regardless, but it was best to keep the wife happy.

"I don't have any money on me at the moment," Grant said.

Tonya laughed at the thought of wanting his money, "You say you're working a case, is that correct?"

"That's correct." Grant looked at her curiously, "Why?"

"I think I know where my wife is going with this," Isaiah said. "See, we've been out here for a long while. You know what I use to do, and you also know she was in the same line of work, that's how we all meet."

"Is there a point to this?" Grant huffed.

"My wife and I want to help you solve the case you're working."

He wasn't too keen on the idea, but he remembered just how good those two were at their jobs. "Can you hack into the Dover police files?" Grant questioned.

"Like taking candy from a baby." Tonya bragged. "Is there a reason?"

"Look for files labeled, "The Midnight Killer." That will fill in the blanks. Tell me if you find anything important. If you need to know anything else ask, Mary."

"That sounds reasonable." Isaiah stood up and walked out of the room, it only took a few minutes for him to return. He slid a phone across the table towards Grant. "Here's the item you wanted. Remember the rules?"

"Don't make any unnecessary calls, only one person can call me and that's you. Most important rule of all, is to throw the phone away after three weeks."

"At least you remember something." Mary laughed.

"Only things of importance." Grant scowled.

Tonya stood from the table, "It's getting late and I'm ready to call it a night. Let me show you to your room young lady."

"I give up," Mary smiled. She turned to look at Grant, "Be careful out there." She bent over and kissed his cheek before following Tonya out of the kitchen.

Isaiah took another drink of his tea keeping a sharp eye on Grant, "How did that young lady get mixed up with you?"

"Long story."

"We have time."

Grant got up from the table, "It's time for me to go. If you want to know anything else ask her." He said walking out of the kitchen towards the exit.

Isaiah followed behind him, "Still running from the past like always."

Grant stopped and turned to face his friend, "My past has already caught up with me," he said. "I just want to keep her safe."

Isaiah cut him off before he could make it to the door, "Are you keeping her safe or yourself?"

"Both." Grant extended his hand to him again, "Thank you for the help."

Isaiah shook his head and grabbed Grant's hand, "I believe this is the first time you've thanked me."

"First time for everything or so I've been told. Let me know what you find in those files."

"Will do. And try to come back in one piece."

"I always do." Grant smirked. He turned walking out of the house, Isaiah watched as he got into his vehicle and drove away.

12

STARTING OVER

ISAIAH WAS SITTING ALONE AT THE KITCHEN TABLE DRINKING HIS TEA and eating a piece of apple pie that his wife had fixed for him before she turned in for the night. Mary couldn't sleep a wink she was worried about, Grant. Instead of tossing and turning she got out of bed and threw on a nightgown that was given to her. She crept down the steps and was going to head outside for a smoke when she caught a glimpse of Isaiah sitting at the kitchen table. She approached him as she would any friend. She was close enough to reach out and touch his shoulder. When he spun around in his chair with a handgun aimed at her head, she let out a shriek of terror.

"Damn girl!" Isaiah hissed. He lowered the gun, but not before scolding her like he would a child, "Don't ever sneak up on a man in the middle of the night that can get you killed ma'am."

"Sorry." She nervously smiled, not that she was going to admit that she peed herself a little.

"Can't sleep?"

"I can't," she answered. "Worried about, Grant."

"The man can take care of himself."

"I know that," she said. "Lately though, he hasn't been acting right. That's what has me worried."

"How well do you know him?" Isaiah questioned.

"We go way back."

"Sounds like along story, might need something to eat for this one," he said. "Would you like something?"

"Why not." She smiled in regards to his kindness.

Isaiah stood from the table and made his way over to the fridge, taking out a pie dish with still half an apple pie left inside, "I've only known Grant for several years." He reached up and opened the cabinet door, grabbing a small plate, "Thing is, he's never mentioned you. Shit, I don't think I know a thing about the man." He walked back to the table and handed the plate over to her.

"Thank you." Mary smiled. "Looks delicious."

"My wife makes the best apple pie in the world," Isaiah said. "Do you mind telling me how you know him?"

"We meet in high school," Mary answered. "Fell in love, moved in together after we graduated."

"What happened?"

"Grant's demons started catching up to him."

"The death of his brother," Isaiah said.

She nodded, "That was the one thing in his life that consumed him. No matter how hard he tried, Grant couldn't let it go. He thought for sure if he headed for New York he could solve his brother's murder. He followed his past and I stayed behind. Haven't seen him in years, then he just shows back up in my life and all hell breaks loose."

"Grant has a way of bringing hell with him wherever he goes." Isaiah frowned.

"I have a question for you," she said. She took a bite of the apple pie, "This is good."

"Told you." Isaiah smirked. He took a bite of apple pie himself and washed it down with a drink of tea. "If I were a gambling man, I would say you want to know more about me and my relationship with Grant."

"You would win that one," Mary said. "Will you tell me?"

His facial expression changed, "You may not like what you hear."

"I'm a big girl."

"Don't say I didn't warn you," he said. "Let me tell you something about, Grant. The man has walked on the other side, a place that most people barely see." Isaiah took a drink of his tea, eyeing Mary over the rim of the cup, "Do you believe in more than what you can see?"

"Are you talking about ghosts?" Mary did her best not to laugh.

"Ghosts, Demons, Aliens, things of that nature." Isaiah wasn't joking, not once did he even crack a smile.

"That's all make believe." She chuckled lightly. What Isaiah had said was slightly funny, though the look on his face was not that of telling a joke. " Wait, are you being serious?"

"Let's just say that I worked cases sort of like that with the government," Isaiah told her.

"Like a man in black kind of thing?" Again she laughed at his words.

"This is no laughing matter ma'am." Isaiah grunted. "There are things that you don't know about in this world. Even now I shouldn't be telling you these things, but it is wise that you know why Grant acts the way he does."

Mary pushed her plate to the side, "Alright Isaiah, I'm listening."

"You see, Tonya and myself meet Grant way back when while working a case. It was supposed to be our very last before we ran off and got married."

"What kind of case?" She asked.

"Young lady you need to learn some patience." He took another drink of his tea, afterward letting out a long sigh, "We were sent to hunt down a cult leader, his name was Timmy Jackson. He had a way of making normal people turn on one another, or making them apart of his crazy little gang. Some believed the man used his mind to control others," Isaiah glanced over at Mary. "But you think what you will. Anyways, the man was a bonafide nut-"

"What does any of this have to do with Grant?" Mary interrupted again.

"Do you want to hear this or not?" Isaiah grumbled. Mary nodded in response, “Then please stop interrupting me when I speak.” She faintly smiled and nodded again. “Timmy Jackson was a damn psycho,” Isaiah continued. “He killed for fun. His followers were just as bad, eager to kill for the man they called a leader. Grant was a part of that cult, or so we thought. He would constantly get in our way, and we would get in his. Hell, it even got to the point we fired on one another.

I still say to this day, Timmy Jackson was playing with our heads but that’s beside the point. Grant was a quick thinking man, came up with the idea to lead us out of town one night, so he could explain himself. Seeing how he was honest with us, we showed him the same respect.

It was Tonya’s idea that we team up and take Timmy down. Though that didn’t go the way she had hoped it would. Don’t get me wrong, we did take Timmy’s group down, but before we could place him in custody. Grant put a bullet right between the man’s eyes, not saying he didn’t have it coming. Still, you can’t just go killing unarmed men in such a way, doesn’t matter how evil they are.

Your man and our later in life friend disappeared just as quickly as he pulled that trigger. Mind you, Tonya wanted him behind bars, made it her life's work to see that happen. As you could imagine we didn’t get to completely retire. Tonya tracked Grant to some small town in Wisconsin, after years of tracking the man we finally had him cornered. What we didn’t expect, was Grant asking for our help. It was then she decided it would be best to help the lesser of two evils. Why? I don’t know. Maybe she felt that what he had told us was the truth. And the person he was after had to be dealt with first.

It took some time, along with a couple of close calls, we took another crazy off the streets. Was he one of those special cases? Not sure, don’t think I will ever know. Just like the last time, Grant killed that person too, a bullet right between the eyes.” Isaiah sighed and finished off his cup of tea.

“So if Grant was such a bad person. Why is he not in jail or prison?” Mary asked with a confused look on her face.

"Never said he was a bad man, he marches to the beat of his own drum is all."

"He was just killing your targets, is that what you're trying to tell me?

"Something like that."

"I don't believe you!" Mary hissed.

"Hear me out, will you. Grant is different then most, he has a certain way about him. Call it a gift if you will, something that allows him to sense evil in other humans. This next part is going to seem strange to you, so take it however you want. Every one of us is born with evil embedded deep down within our souls. Some of us ignore it, while others choose to embrace it, let that evil fester inside like a virus. Those are the ones that lose themselves, take on a different form if you will.

They get to the point where they feel nothing for their brothers and sisters of the world. Pain and suffering are all they know, it's the only thing that makes them feel alive, gets them off. Those are the ones that Grant can sense out of all the others, the ones that he kills without mercy. I'm not saying it's right, but after all the years of chasing people like that. I learned that not everyone can be saved, nor do they need to be. He takes that evil out of this world before more innocent lives are lost, is what that man does." Isaiah yawned stretching his arms high into the air.

"Do you think he would kill an innocent?" Mary questioned

"No, and neither do you. Grant is driven by the demons of his past, the very same demons that gave him that gift that I told you about. He's a good man, remember that if nothing more, that's why he's a free man. His work is important and far from done, and we will help him anyway that we can." Isaiah stood from his chair, "If you will excuse me, I am going to call it a night, I suggest you do the same."

"Can I ask you something, Isaiah?"

"I see no reason why you can't."

"Do you know what he went through to get this so-called gift?"

"Yes ma'am I do. Though that is not a tale that I wish to share, not even with you."

"Why is that?" Mary asked, surprised that he refused to she that part of the story.

"Grant is the only one that can tell you what you want to know," Isaiah answered. "Not me." He walked away and disappeared into the darkness of the house. Mary sat in the kitchen by herself for a while longer before calling it a night.

Clouds covered the morning sky cooling down what would be the usual hot summer day. Grant had already dumped the red beater car in favor of a nicer blue truck. He was on his way back to where it all started for him, the very first night he rolled back into his hometown. He felt as though he might have missed something that night. As it was Lieutenant Harris's crime scene he happened upon. To do a proper exam of the crime scene he needed his full concentration.

There were too many reporters and onlookers causing a distraction. On top of that he learned a lot from Harris and seen no need to interfere. Grant now came to the conclusion that he was wrong in his assumption and wanted to perform his own crime scene examination. He pulled the vehicle over into the alleyway where that poor bastard hung that rainy night. Unfortunately, the side of the building had been cleaned so he didn't have any blood splatter patterns to go by.

Next, he scoured the ground around the building, to see if Harris may have missed something. There was a powdery substance, reminding him of drugs of course, along with a few rose petals scattered in some of the areas that caught his attention. Makes sense to find these here, the killers must have been rushed in some way, causing them to drop the rose petals. Which is why they followed Dan and me to the morgue to finish what they started. But how does any of this tie back to Harris having the keys to the morgue. Especially when he claimed he was jumped from behind and the keys were taken? Grant thought to himself.

One thing that was clear in fact, the killers had planned on finishing up with the body in that very spot. And wasn't expecting to be interrupted. Though who or what caught them off guard? Was it Harris and he turned a blind eye? Or perhaps the killers have something on him? He quickly shrugged any types of thoughts like that off. He made up his mind that the murderers were caught off guard and had to act fast. If he can find out who made the call to the police station about the body, he can also find out what else they may have seen.

Only that wasn't going to happen until Isaiah hacks the police station computers and gets a hold of those files. It was a waiting game at the moment, and while Grant waited he was going to look for more clues. He needed to make his next move, his plan was to get back into the morgue. He wanted to take a closer look at the body of, Leonard Clifton. It damn sure wasn't going to be easy. Since Harris was no threatening to throw his ass in jail if he was caught meddling in police affairs again. Which meant he could only rely on one person, Officer Turner.

As much as he hated the thought of asking that slimy man any favors, he realized there wasn't much of a choice in the matter. Grant sighed and picked up the phone he got from, Isaiah. He dialed the number to the police precinct, hoping that anyone other than that bitch of a lady answered the phone.

"Dover Police station," an old man answered. "How can I help you?"

"Thank god," Grant mumbled to himself.

"Excuse me?"

"Nothing," Grant said quickly. "Is Officer Turner in today?"

"Let me check." The man placed him on hold for several minutes.

"This is Officer Turner, may I ask who is calling?"

"It's me, Grant."

"What do you want, Dawson?" Turner sounded frustrated, yet had a bit of intrigue to his voice.

Grant took a deep breath, "I need you to get me back into the city morgue. It sickens me, but the only person I can ask for help is you."

"Nice way to ask for someone's help." Turner grumbled. "Why do you need back in there?"

"Needing to look over Leonard Clifton's body."

"Well Dawson, I'm afraid I can't do that," Turner replied.

"Why the hell not!" Grant shouted into the phone.

"Because it wouldn't do you any good. Harris already had the body cremated."

"Damn it!" Grant slammed his hand on the hood of the truck out of anger. "Why in the hell would he do that the body still held clues!"

"Your guess is as good as mine." Turner went silent on the other end. Grant was about to hang up the phone when he began speaking again. "I need to show you something."

"Not this again."

"It's not like that."

"Then what?" Grant questioned.

"Do you trust me?" Turner responded.

"Can't trust a man that I don't like."

"Feeling is mutual." Turner retorted. "Look, if we're going to help each other out then we need to find some common ground. This case is bigger than both of us and right now. Like or not we're the only ones that seem to still want it solved. So how about we put our hatred for each other aside and get this damn mess cleaned up."

Grant didn't want to admit it but the man was right, "What do you have in mind?"

"Meet me at the morgue in twenty minutes, don't be late." After Turner said what he had to say he hung up the phone.

Twenty minutes later Grant arrived at the morgue, Turner was sitting in his car waiting. The young officer got out of his car first and slowly approached. Both men casually walked through the doors into the morgue. Inside they were approached by a young lady with brown hair and pink glasses. "Officer Turner." She smiled, "To what do we owe this visit?"

Turner slapped Grant on the back, "This here is Officer Dawson, he's the new rookie in town. Need to show him around the morgue, you know to get his feet wet."

"Shouldn't you take him to the coroner's office first?" She laughed.

Tuner wagged his finger in front of her face, "I know what I'm doing, Lacey. And you don't have to keep calling me Officer Turner, Randy is fine."

"Officer Turner suits you better. Have fun showing him the dead people."

"Cute." Grant smirked.

"Don't say a word." Turner warned him.

"Not going to, I mean who I am I to stop young love."

"You're not funny." Turner bumped into Grant walking past him, "What I want to show you is this way." He had Grant follow him to the back of the morgue, "I hid a body in here with Lacey's help." He opened up one of the fridge doors where the bodies are kept fresh. Turner reached down and pulled out a metal table with a black body bag on it.

"Does Harris know about this?" Grant questioned.

"I prefer he didn't."

"There has to be a reason you're keeping this from him."

"About that." Turner raised his brow. "Harris had ordered this body be destroyed, just like Leonard Clifton's."

"For what reason?" Grant asked.

"Only one reason I can think of," he replied. "This is another victim of the murderer."

"That can't be."

"Stop acting surprised. This happened a few days ago, I tried to call you but you never answered."

"I was busy," Grant said.

"None of my business and I don't care," Turner replied. "Go ahead, take a look for yourself, that is why I brought you here."

Grant reached over and unzipped the body bag. Seeing the body sent a chill down his back, as he suspected it was another young lady. Though this lady looked a lot like Mary, almost the spitting image of her to be exact. Something was different about this murder. There were no signs of the victim being tortured, and that was usually the killers calling card. She wasn't dressed up or stripped of her clothing. And the victim was heinously beaten to death with a blunt object. Who knows if the lady was targeted like the other victims or if something triggered the attack.

"Where did you find the body?" Grant questioned.

"Dumped on the side of the road like trash." It was hard for the young cop to view the body again, let alone think about how the body was disposed of.

"Who called it in?"

"Some lady."

"Did she see anything?" Grant asked, even though his gut told him Hera made the call after she killed the girl.

"It's a little shady," Turner said. "The lady claimed that a slim figured person jumped out of a black van. Then threw the body out of the passenger side before jumping back in the vehicle."

"Anything else?"

"Not that I know of."

Grant ran his fingers through his hair, "I'm going to need the name of the witness."

"Why?" Turner responded with a question of his own.

"Why else, I need to question them myself. Is that a problem?"

"Problem is she didn't leave a name."

"Damn." Grant sighed.

"Right, you don't need to draw more attention to yourself at this point," Turner said.

"Maybe there is no need to question the witness."

"Why is that?"

"Slim figured person dressed in a weird outfit, it's got to be a woman," Grant answered.

"You can't make that assumption just by that description alone," Turner said. "To me, that means you're hiding something."

"How perceptive of you." Grant's brow furrowed, "Some information is private and on a need to know basis."

Turner got in his face, "Well I need to know, I scratched your back now you need to return the favor."

Grant laughed at how the officer was reacting, "Ease up tough guy," he said. "Like I said before, I don't like you, but I do need help from someone on the inside. Seeing how you shared this with me, allow me to share this with you." He gave him a brief description of the events that had transpired over the past few weeks. It was a shocking bit of information, and Turner wasn't sure how to handle it.

"Is Mary okay?" Turner questioned.

"She's safe now." Grant reassured him.

"Can I speak with her?"

"That's not going to happen," Dawson responded. "She's with a friend of mine, that's all that anyone needs to know. Until this whole thing is over, that's how it's got to be."

Turner thought about it for a second and came to the conclusion that Grant was doing the right thing, "I will see what I can dig up on the things you have told me. Not sure what your next move will be, nor do I care to know. Stay out of trouble, tell nobody of what I showed you today."

13

GETTING CLOSER TO THE TRUTH

HOURS LATER GRANT FOUND HIMSELF BACK AT THE FLOWER SHOP THAT he visited a couple of weeks ago. This time however he went in with a different approach, he demanded to see the list of people that buy, Japanese Roses. The last time he tried using the nice guy routine, he was refused. Though the girl working was nice enough to give him some information just not all he sought. This time he threatened to have the place shut down if his demands were not met.

With the owner there, it was only a matter of time before he was given what he wanted. He thanked them and promised to return the buyers list once he looked it over. He walked out of the flower shop and made his way over to the coffee place across the street. Grant took a seat, ordered a cup of coffee, black, no sugar. He began to glance over the list of people that have bought the roses.

He was caught off guard by how many people have purchased that type of flower. The girl that worked the counter that day had lied to him, but for what reason. Grant had a feeling the young lady was protecting the store that she worked for, not trying to protect one of the buyers. The list was long indeed, by the time he found what he was looking for, he had drank three cups of coffee. As he read on a single name caught his attention, Christy. No last name, no address, no other information except for the dates of purchases made. Every time this woman's name popped up, it coincided with every murder.

The information was helpful, but it was very doubtful that the lady would give her real name. Though it surprised him that the name Hera wasn't used as the alias. The name Christy must have some sort of significance to one of the killers. Grant paid for the coffee and tipped the waitress, he walked back across the street towards the flower shop. He did as he said and returned the list of buyers to the owner of the store.

Grant was sitting in his truck deciding on his next move when his phone rang, "Hope you have good news for me, Isaiah," he answered.

"If hacking into the police files is good news, then yeah guess I do," Isaiah responded on the other end of the line.

Hearing that brought a smile to his face, it's possible he could be one step closer to solving the case. "Find out anything interesting?" Grant asked.

"More than what I expected to find. The Dover police station has more secrets than our very own government."

"Most do Isaiah," Grant said. "Did you happen to find the files I asked of?"

"Of course what am I an amateur?"

"What did you find?"

"Looks like a man named Harris has had his hands all over this case of yours," Isaiah said. "Some files have been deleted though, unfortunately I couldn't recover those. What I did find out are things I'm sure you already know. Evidence wise, Japanese Rose petals found at the crime scenes, how the victims were dressed, how some were put in certain positions-"

"What about a powdery substance being found?" Grant interrupted. "I'm almost certain it was cocain."

"Nothing like that is in these files."

"Hmm, does anything seem out of the ordinary?"

"There was one file that I saved from being deleted," Isaiah said.

"And?" This was the best news he had heard all day, considering what he had seen at the morgue.

"No names are mentioned, but it does say something about a lady taken to an asylum. By the hospital reports though, it doesn't seem like she was in need of such treatment. So why go through all the trouble of having her institutionalized?"

"That's the million dollar question," Grant said. "And I'm going to find the answer."

"How are you going to manage that?" Isaiah questioned.

"By going to the asylum. Can you do me another favor?"

"What do you need?"

"Did you happen to see any of Harris's personal files?"

"Haven't looked," Isaiah answered.

"Take a look, see what you can find and give me a callback." Grant insisted.

"Will do, take care of yourself out there."

"Thanks, Isaiah," Grant replied, then hung up the phone.

Grant pulled his vehicle up at the asylum he had already visited once before. He went in with one agenda, to talk with Grace Jones once more. He didn't ask for assistance, he made his way straight for Grace's room. Grant barged into her room, but she wasn't there. He pulled one of the nurses to the side and asked for assistance. The answer he received was one that was unexpected. Grant was informed that Grace had been taken from the facility.

When he asked why nobody had a straight answer for him. What he could gather was that a man claiming to be an officer of the law came and picked her up. Which from what he was told, happened at least three or four times a month. Not good, Grant thought to himself. Two criminals, one man, one woman. That would match up with Mary's story. That meant what he was thinking all along was correct, one of the killers was definitely a cop. There was this sickening feeling building in the pit of his stomach. One last question that he needed to ask would confirm his feeling.

"I need to speak with Grace's doctor? I believe he or she will have the rest of the answers I am after," Grant said.

"Of course." The nurse walked away and came back with the head doctor.

"Can I help you?" The doctor asked, it was a lady with long gray hair, tall and thin stature. Her facial features said that she was a no-nonsense kind of woman.

"Yes, my name is-" Grant was trying to say.

"Don't bother, I remember you from before," the doctor said. "Also, you're not an actual cop. Nurse see him to the door."

"Wait!" He held up his hands, "This time is different. Grace could be in danger, I need to know who took her."

"The same cop that comes to pick her up every two or three weeks," the doctor replied.

"I need his name!" Grant demanded.

"Officer Bryant," she answered.

"Can I see the time he has come before?"

"Do you have a search warrant?" She glared daggers at him when she asked that question.

"This is serious!" Grant snarled. "I don't know if you've been keeping up with the news way out here. But there is a killer out there, and Grace is either in danger, or she's involved with the murders somehow." He had a stern look on his face to make what he was going to say next more believable, "All I have to do is make one phone call to my friend, and cops will be swarming this place. Got what I'm saying here?"

The doctor looked on nervously, "I can't give you documents without a warrant." Little beads of sweat were forming above her brow, "Off the record though. I will say that she has gone missing several times in the past. A couple months ago, afterward she went missing in the middle of the year. Last month it was towards the end, you can figure out the rest."

"And you didn't see fit to inform anyone?"

"Who am I going to tell? She's a former drug addict with no friends or family."

"What about the police?" Grant responded, not giving what he said much of a thought.

“Like we’ve been telling you, it was a male cop that picks her up each time,” the lady said.

“Give me a description of the man! And be quick about it!”

The doctor took out a small rag, wiping the sweat from her forehead, “The man was dressed like a cop, from the shoes to the hat on his head. He had salt and pepper hair, about your height just a little heavier. But he never revealed his eyes, always had a pair of sunglasses on. Oh, and he only picked Grace up at night.” She gave the best description she could.

“Thank you for the information, I will be out of your hair. And I promise that won’t be back.”

Grant left the asylum with a new found purpose, he had a target now and it was time to do a little background check. Either she was the female killer that went by, Hera. Or she was in more trouble than anyone realized. He had two options, he could call and ask Turner for help or he could get a hold of Isaiah. He refused to deal with the officer for the second time, so he called up Isaiah for another favor.

“What do you need now?” Isaiah answered the phone. “Wait, wait, wait, let me guess. You need another favor.”

“Still trying to find a sense of humor I see,” he said. “In all seriousness though, I need you to look up a name for me.”

“This is going to interfere with the other thing you asked me to do.”

“Right now that’s not important.”

“This is?” Isaiah questioned.

“Very,” Grant said with urgency.

Things got quite on the other end for a minute or two, “If that’s what you want. Give me the name,” he said.

“Grace Jones.”

“What makes this lady so important?”

“The killer I’ve been chasing for the past few weeks let her live a few years back,” Grant answered. “Afterwards she was instituted by one the officers on call the night she was attacked.”

“The lady being talked about in the police files.”

"What makes matters worse, I think the killer has been paying visits to her ever since."

"With her being as traumatized as she was that night, plus meds on top of that. The murderer can easily get inside her head, making Grace believe that he spared her life for a reason," Isaiah said.

"Which means she believes that her second chance should be used to serve him. I was contemplating that she may be in grave danger but now-" Grant paused mid-sentence.

"You think you found the identity of the second killer. Right?" Isaiah replied.

"I believe so, that's why I need you to see if she has any family near the area. If I can have a word with someone that knows her, maybe I can figure out a way to draw her out in the open."

"Let me see what I can do," Isaiah said. Grant could hear his fingers punching the keys of his laptop, "Hmm, says here Grace was born in the small town of, Kirby. Her dad died when she was eight years of age, doesn't really say from what though. No brothers or sisters, looks like her mother wasn't the nicest of people. Grace was taken to the hospital multiple times for injuries, the doctor believed abuse to be the cause.

Looking through her arrest records now, man did this girl start at an early age. She was in trouble with the law at the ripe age of thirteen, spent most of her teen years in the system. Drugs, theft, extreme violence towards her peers, you name it this girl did it."

"What type of violence?" Grant asked.

"The bullying type stuff, beating up other teens, mainly girls," Isaiah responded. "Just in case you're wondering, and I'm sure you are. The mother is still alive and well and still lives in Kirby. Lucky for you that's only twenty miles out."

"One more thing." Grant paused. "How's Mary holding up?"

"She's doing good, helping Tonya out around the house shit like that. Still seems to be having trouble sleeping at night, but can you blame her?" Isaiah told him. "Asking questions about you, and why Tonya acts like she doesn't know who you are."

He let out a long slow breath, "What have you told her?"

"Don't worry haven't told her the important things. Whatever you do, don't blame yourself. Feelings like that will only distract you from the bigger picture. And you know what that does to someone like us."

"I do," Grant said before hanging up the phone.

Dawson arrived in Kirby thirty minutes later after getting off the phone with, Isaiah. This was the first time he had ever been in the town, it was small and quaint, not too friendly on the eyes either. He remembered from his childhood, his father and brother coming here to fish. Grant never got the chance to go when he came of age, with what happened to his brother and all. After that his family fell apart, his father never cared for fishing anymore. His mom just stayed to herself, barely leaving the house.

He pulled up to an old run down house, trash was scattered all around the yard. Junked up car parts and other pieces of machinery laid about the house, it looked like a hoarder lived there. Grant went up to the door and knocked, he stood there waiting for someone to answer the door. It took several tries before the door slowly opened. An older lady peeked her head outside.

"Who are you?" The lady hissed. "Are you another one of those damn door to door salesman?"

"No, ma'am," he replied. "My name is, Grant Dawson." If he told her he was just an investigator, then she would just shut the door in his face, "I'm a detective with the Dover county police force. I'm here to talk with about your daughter, Grace Jones."

"I don't have a daughter!"

"Miss Jones." Grant began.

"My name is, Audrey."

"Okay, Audrey. Grace is in a bit of trouble and I need your help."

"She was always troubled from the day she was born."

"How so?" Grant questioned.

Audrey opened the door and waived Grant on in, "Don't just stand there, come on in." He walked inside the house, it was just as bad as the outside. He could barely walk without tripping over boxes of clutter, "Would you like some tea?" She turned and asked. "Or maybe some vodka instead?"

"No thank you." He kindly refused. "I just need some information, that's all. Then I will be out of your hair."

Audrey laughed, "You cops are all the same, stick in the mud. If you don't mind I will have some tea and vodka." She went to the kitchen and mixed herself a drink, then came back in the room where Grant stood waiting. "Ask your questions then get out of my house, the smell of pig dampens the place."

"Always liked being called a pig." Grant joked. "About your daughter."

"I don't have a daughter." Audrey claimed yet again.

"Then what is she to you if not a daughter?"

"A curse!" She grumbled. "A curse to me, a curse to her father, a damn curse to everyone that comes in contact with her."

"Why say that about your own child?"

She took a drink of her tea and vodka, "She killed her own father."

"She was only eight when her father died. How could that be her fault?" Grant asked, trying to contain his anger towards this drunk that stood before him.

"Because she lived and he died!" Audrey shouted, spilling some of her tea.

"And you beat her for that every day of her young life!" He shouted back, somewhat losing his composure.

"How else would you deal with a child such as her?" She calmly responded before taking another drink.

Grant took a deep breath to calm his nerves, "I didn't come here to question you about past discretions." He cleared his throat. "Tell me about her teen years."

"Not much to tell," Audrey replied. "She was a troublemaker, hurting others was her thing."

"Who did she target the most?"

"Girls her own age," she said. "Mainly the cheerleader type, blond, thin, nice looking and popular." She finished off her glass of tea and vodka. Audrey looked back at Grant, "Do you have any more questions for me?"

"No, that will do," he said.

"Then get the hell out of my house!" Audrey demanded. She stumbled her way back into the kitchen and out of sight.

There was no need for him to stay any longer, he had seen and heard enough to know why Grace was so violent. But she wasn't the one in control, the one that calls himself Hades was. So unless Grant could figure out a way to break her away from him, then he will never be able to draw her out. Though after talking with Audrey, he came up with the perfect way to get under Grace's skin. The problem with the plan he had in mind, he would need Mary's help to pull it off.

Grant would need a couple more items from the hotel he stayed at before all hell broke loose. He walked inside and made his way to the front desk, "Can I help you?" the clerk asked.

"Let's hope so. I was staying here a few nights ago and I think I may have left some things in my room," he said. "I was checking to see if housekeeping may have turned anything in."

"Name?"

"Grant Dawson."

"Well, Mr. Dawson. Housekeeping hasn't been in your room since you've been away, by your request of course," the clerk said. "If you need something out of your room, by all means go and retrieve it. After all you paid for a full month."

"Thank you for the help."

"Of course, Mr. Dawson." The clerk smiled in return.

Grant walked up the steps to the second floor like nothing was wrong, though in the back of his mind he was afraid that a trap laid in wait for him. He kept his hand on the holster of his gun, inching his way forward. He stood in front of the door to his room now, to this point nothing had happened. He reached for the doorknob turned it, pushing the door forward. The lights were on in the room, Grant was sure he had turned them off. This made him draw his gun before entering.

He cautiously walked inside the room, he wasn't attacked by the killers nor did anything blow up. But what he saw inside the room, backed up his notion that he was doing the right thing. Pictures of Mary were hung all over the walls in the room. Though it didn't end there, the eyes of each picture had been removed. Which proved just how much Grace hated Mary, Grant guessed it was because Hades refused to cause harm to her. He didn't stand around looking for much longer, he quickly grabbed the cellphones from the bed. Took his bag of goodies and shoved the phones inside and bolted out the door.

The sun was beginning to set as Grant was making his way back to Isaiah's place out in the woods. He pushed the gas pedal down harder causing the truck to speed down the darkened highway. He needed to rush if he was to make sure another innocent would not be harmed. Grant pulled the truck up to the front of the log home and rushed inside the house.

"What the hell!" Isaiah shouted.

Grant held up his hands, "Hey wait! It's me don't shoot!"

"Damn it man!" Isaiah snarled. "What the hell is wrong with you?"

"I need help." Grant was breathing hard.

"Haven't I been doing enough?"

"Not from you," he said as he gasped for air. "This time I need Mary's help."

About that time Mary walked around the corner, "What are you doing here?" She asked.

"He needs your help," Tonya said, walking past her and over by Isaiah. "Am I right, Grant?"

"I need Mary's help now more than ever."

"You drop me off here, pretend like I don't exist, and now you all of a sudden need my help." Mary's upper lip started to tremble, she was indeed angry with his actions.

"The one that called herself Hera, hates your guts. You made that very clear when you spoke of the way she treated you. I believe that she would do anything, and I mean anything to see you dead." Grant explained. "And because of that I think we can draw her out."

"Why would she want to still kill me?"

"You took something from her." Grant answered.

"I didn't take anything from her," Mary said.

"You did." Grant insisted. "The attention given to her by Hades, she views him as a father figure. Seeing how her own father was killed when she was eight after that her life was hell."

"That's horrible." She frowned. "But why take it out on me?"

"Not sure." He shrugged. "From what I've been told she has always hated blondes, especially ones she viewed as popular."

"So you know who she is?" Her eyes widened at the possibility.

"Her name is, Grace Jones," Grant replied.

"That name sounds familiar." Tonya butted in.

"She was the only one to survive when the murders first started," Mary answered. "I can't believe that it would be her though."

"And why not?" Isaiah responded. "Most children that come from abusive homes and have trauma in their adult life. Can make them easy prey to someone of a stronger will."

"Can you protect her if you put her in that kind of danger?" Tonya questioned.

"I can and I will," Grant said with confidence.

"I can take care of myself!" Mary said with pride in her voice. "The days of needing someone to protect or take care of me are over." She looked over at Grant, "What do you want me to do?"

Before Grant could answer his cell phone began to ring, "Just as I planned." He smirked. "Answer this." He held out the phone for Mary to take

She took the phone from his hand holding it up to her ear, "Hello?"

"Is this who I think it is," a female voice said in return.

"It depends on who you're looking for," Mary replied.

"That sweet little thing I had fun with not too long ago." The woman laughed.

"Fuck you!"

The woman kept laughing, then all went silent. "I want to kill you," she said in a low creepy voice.

"You tried before and failed to get the job done." She chuckled, trying her best to piss off the woman on the other end of the line.

"True." She agreed. "Not through lack of trying, that investigator friend of yours is good. But I doubt he can save you from me again."

"How about we find out," Mary responded with some arrogance. "Tell me where to meet you and we can finish this nonsense."

"Will your boyfriend be there?" She playfully asked.

"It will be just you and me."

"You've got some brass, I will give you that. First prissy woman I've had to stand up to me, but you suck at lying. Tell you a secret, I want him to be with you. It will be fun to see his face when he watches you die." The woman started singing some incoherent words to herself.

"Stop acting like a crazy person and give me an address!" Mary demanded.

That snapped the woman out of her trance-like state of mind, "Meet me at the end of town, it's about forty miles out. Your boyfriend knows the place he's been before. Oh and dear, I'm not acting." There was a click and then nothing after that.

"Well?" Grant said.

"She wants us to meet her out of town, she said you will know the place," Mary replied.

Grant's brow furrowed, "The old shoe factory."

"That creepy old building on the outskirts of town." Mary frowned.

"The one and only," Grant said. "Last time I was out there things didn't go so well."

"What happened?" She asked.

"They had their own torture chamber waiting for me," he answered. "Who knows what she will have waiting for us."

"One way to find out," Mary replied.

"Then let's go." Grant motioned. "Times wasting, if she leaves before we get there we won't get a second chance."

Tonya slipped Mary a hunting knife still in its sheath, "Keep this close for protection," she whispered.

"Thank you," Mary whispered back.

"Grant you know I don't need to tell you this, but try not to die." Isaiah smirked. "You still owe me, and I intend to collect."

Grant nodded, "Can't die yet, still have plenty of work that needs to be completed," he said. Grant smiled at Mary and turned to leave, she ran up beside him and took his hand in hers.

14

NOT OVER UNTIL IT'S OVER

It was eleven thirty at night and the rain was coming down when Grant and Mary pulled up at the old shoe factory. Last time he was there, he had to crawl underneath the fence, this time around the gate was left open. Of course that would be the case, since they are being welcomed into the murders world yet again. Grant loaded his gun and threw a couple more magazines in his pockets.

Grant and Mary walked up to the steel double doors that allowed them inside the factory. Mary was the one that pushed on the doors, and with a loud creaking noise that could be heard throughout, the doors slowly opened.

"This is it," he whispered. "Once we walk inside there is no turning back. You can still back out, I wouldn't blame you if you did."

"I want to do this," Mary said. "Whoever these people are, they need to be stopped. No one else needs to die, let's end this."

He was taken aback by how far Mary had come, she was no longer that frail girl he remembered from his past. "At least take this." Grant offered her a gun but she refused to take it. He had forgotten that guns weren't her thing, she hated them since childhood. "Then stay close to me," he told her.

"Okay." Mary smiled. "Ready when you are."

They cautiously walked inside the factory, there was no need for flashlights as the place was dimly lit. Question was, where was Grace Jones hiding? Grant called out but didn't use her name, as to make sure he didn't chase her away. Then he had Mary call out to her, that's when laughter filled the building.

"So glad you two could join me!" Grace's voice echoed.

"Follow me and stay close," Grant said to Mary. They both walked the narrow halls of the shoe factory. The search so far was proving fruitless, though it would seem Grace was getting closer to them. They could hear the pitter-patter of feet, and she was banging on the walls with what sounded like a steel pipe. "She's close," he whispered.

"Look." Mary pointed.

"Look at what? I don't see any-" Grant paused mid-sentence. For a second he thought he saw something moving in the shadows. A moment later he could see movement again. Then out of the shadows, a figure appeared before them, dressed in some freakishly weird outfit. "My name is Grant Dawson, I am a private investigator! Come quietly and no one has to get hurt!" He shouted. The figure stood there tilting its head back and forth, "If you don't cooperate, I will have no other choice but to use force! Do you understand?"

Grant was trying to talk some sense into who he believed was, Grace Jones. In an instant the figure bolted forward, "Stop now! Don't make me shoot you!" He warned. "Grace, stop this madness! It's over!" Grace didn't give him a choice, she was charging at them with a knife in hand. Grant fired three rounds, each hitting its target. Grace went down and wasn't moving.

"Is she dead?" Mary gasped.

"Stay here while I check it out." He left Mary behind approaching Grace cautiously. Grant knelt down beside her, deciding to reach for the mask that covered her face. He grabbed the mask and pulled it off her head, revealing that it wasn't who he had thought. Instead of it being Grace Jones behind the mask, it was in fact her mother, Audrey Jones. "What the hell?"

"Grant!" Mary screamed out all of a sudden. He turned to see that another person wearing a costume had a hold of Mary from behind with a knife to her throat.

"Thought you were so smart," Grace said. "But you made a mistake thinking I would be here alone." She laughed.

"Don't do anything stupid, Grace!" Grant shouted at her.

Grace pulled off her mask and tossed it on the floor, "Guess I don't need that thing anymore."

"We know you've been the one killing people," he said. "The games end here. Now put the knife down and let her go!"

"I'm afraid I can't do that," she replied.

"You can and you will!" He demanded.

"No!" Grace screamed. "This isn't over until she's dead! And then you die! After that he will love me again, he will see that I'm his favorite. Not her!" Grace went to slit Mary's throat.

"No!!" Grant shouted. Gunshots echoed throughout the building, Mary shrieked, and Grace dropped the knife and collapsed to the floor. Grant went running over to her, "Are you alright?" He asked her. Mary mumbled a few incoherent words, she was in complete shock. He pulled her into a warm embrace. He was happy to see that she was safe, but if he didn't fire the shots at Grace then who did?

It was then that the now Captain Harris walked from the shadows and into the light. "I always seem to be saving your ass lately." Harris chuckled, as he put his gun back into his holster. Grant stood there looking astonished.

"How did you know that we were here?" Grant questioned.

"thank you first would be nice," Harris said.

"Thank you," Grant finally said. "Still, how did you know?"

"I was keeping tabs on you." Harris didn't look at Grant when he spoke, instead he stared down at Grace with a look of sorrow in his eyes. "So this is the so-called Midnight Killer?"

Grant noticed the look on his friend's face, "Did you know her?"

The Captain looked back up at Grant, "Not really," he said. "Who is she again?"

"Grace Jones," Grant answered.

"You can let me go now," Mary whispered in Grant's ear. He had completely forgotten that he was holding her in his arms.

"Sorry, Mary." Grant nervously laughed.

"It's alright." Mary smiled in return.

Harris pushed through the middle of them both, making his way over to the other body on the floor. "Who in the hell is she?"

"That's Grace's mother, Audrey Jones," Grant responded, kind of caught off guard with how Harris was still acting like an asshole.

"After all these years I thought I was chasing a single man. And here it turns out to be a couple of fucking women." Harris spat.

"It would seem so," Grant said.

"Oh well." Harris shrugged. He walked over and patted Grant on the back, "Next time fill me in on when you're going to do something stupid." Then he looked over at Mary, "Guess you can rest easy now that these two crazies have been dealt with."

"Guess so." She faintly smiled.

Harris got on his radio and called for backup, "We've got this from here on out." Other cops started flooding the scene, "Will someone kindly show these two out."

"No need," Grant said. "We're leaving. I think we've had enough for one night." He took Mary's hand in his and they walked out of the factory together.

The next day Grant and Mary woke up in the same bed after sharing an intimate night together. That moment though wasn't going to last. Grant was destined to walk a different path. While Mary loved the hometown life that she had built for herself so far. Grant had already dressed and made his way downstairs, joining Isaiah and Tonya at the table for breakfast. Mary came down minutes later and joined them at the table as well. After a quiet breakfast Tonya broke the silence.

"What are you going to do now that the case has been solved?" Tonya asked Grant.

"Head back home," he answered. "I still have more work to be done."

"How does that make you feel Mary?" Tonya questioned.

"Tonya!" Isaiah grunted. "What do you think you're doing?"

"Whatever do you mean dear?" She smirked.

"It's alright Isaiah," Mary said. "I know that Grant's not staying, that's why we wanted to spend one last night together."

"I'm sorry Mary." Grant frowned. "Even if I wanted to I just can't."

"I understand." Mary smiled. "There's no need to explain things to me."

Grant still had this look of wonder and possible confusion on his face. He might of been at the table talking but his mind was elsewhere. Even Mary looked as though she was thinking hard about something important as well.

"You two alright?" Isaiah questioned.

"I just feel like I'm missing something," Grant said, twiddling his thumbs.

"The case is over, both killers were dealt with." Isaiah reassured him.

"It would seem that way." Grant agreed. "But what about the one that went by Hades?"

"It was Audrey pretending to be a man," Tonya said.

"Hades was a man that much I'm sure of," Mary said.

"Something else is bothering you isn't their girl?" Tonya insisted.

Mary stared out the kitchen window, the warm sun beaming through down on her face. "It was something Harris said to me at the factory after he saved my life."

"What did he say?" Grant impatiently asked.

"He said, now that those two have been dealt with you can rest easy," Mary replied. "Harris knew what had happened to me, I know it, the look on his face said as much."

"I didn't tell him," Grant said with haste. "Didn't feel like I could trust him at that time."

Isaiah's computers began to act up, beeping loud enough that everyone in the room jumped. "Never can get used to that damn computer of yours, Isaiah." Tonya grumbled. "Still makes me jump to this day."

"Never heard a computer do that before." Mary added.

"Me either." Grant chimed in.

"Everyone breath it's nothing to fuss over." Isaiah smirked. "It's just letting me know my work is complete."

"You mean?" Grant gasped.

Isaiah stood from the table and walked over to his desk taking a seat. "Let's see what we can find out about the new Captain of the police force." Grant walked over and stood behind Isaiah as he fired up the computer. It took him several days to crack the password, but he had managed to get into the Captain's private files. "First let me say, Harris is a smart man. Took me forever to get past all the firewalls and password protection codes, and all that crazy shit. He's almost as good as me, almost."

"Pull up his files." Grant was in hurry to see what his old mentor was trying so hard to protect.

Isaiah typed a few things on the keyboard, in a matter of seconds the screen lit up with all kinds of information on. Out of everything they skimmed over one thing in particular stood out from the rest. It was an old newspaper article that read, "We are saddened by the news of Christy Harris's passing, daughter of our beloved Officer Harris. We wish him and his wife the best in their time of grieving. Donations will be taken at Dover High, where Christy was a straight A student and loved by her peers. Again this is a sad day for us all."

"I had no idea he lost his daughter." He had a sense of sadness for his old friend. It was a tragedy that few can say they have experienced in their lifetime. Though things such as that has a way of changing a person, and not for the good.

"Also says she was hit by a drunk driver outside a gas station. On her way home for the holidays, man that's fucked up. She died a week later at the Dover Hospital. Not much longer after that his wife passed away."

"Any dates of their deaths?" Grant asked.

"Looks like Harris had the dates removed," Isaiah responded.

"How is that possible?"

"Why the look of surprise? I said your friend was good."

Grant rubbed his chin, "Let me think, let me think. What about a time of death?"

"His daughter died at midnight to be exact," Isaiah answered. "Does that mean anything to you, Grant?" He turned and asked.

"Son of a bitch!" Grant ran out the door without speaking another word, Mary gave chase but he was already in his vehicle speeding away.

"Where is he going in such a hurry?" Mary sighed, watching helplessly as he drove away.

Isaiah walked outside joining her on the porch and Tonya stood behind him, "He put the pieces of the puzzle together," he told Mary.

"He goes to serve justice to the guilty," Tonya said.

Grant was speeding his way down the highway topping speeds of over ninety miles an hour. He was closing in on the police station when from his right an overly large truck came out of nowhere. Hitting the side of his vehicle with a loud thud. The impact was so great that it knocked him unconscious. When the police arrived at the scene both Grant and the person that hit his vehicle had vanished without a trace. The only thing that was left behind was the wrecked truck.

Later that night Grant woke up to find himself in a dimly lit room, tied to a chair yet again. "Ah I see that you're awake." A large figure walked out of the darkness and into the light. Wearing the costume he had seen before, all black with glowing red eyes.

Grant was battered and bruised, maybe even had a few broken ribs. "Hades I presume," he said. Hell, it even hurts to talk.

"Why call me that when you know my real name?" The person answered.

"Harris." Grant snarled, "A man that I once called a friend."

Hades pulled the mask from his face, revealing that he was indeed, Captain Harris. "I thought for sure I had all my bases covered, guess I was wrong. Should have known that making Audrey the fall guy was going to come back to bite me on the ass."

"In the process you got your protege killed." Grant laughed.

"She wasn't my protege!" Harris snapped

"Then what was she to you? A lackey? Or was she was more like a daughter to you? The daughter you lost."

"What would you know!" Harris screamed, slapping Grant across the face.

"I know that your daughter was hit by a drunk driver, I know that she passed away. Not long after that your wife died. I also know that you began killing innocent people at midnight, which was the time of Christy's death. Then you show the world what you feel by what you do with the bodies afterward. On top of that, you think you will gain your daughter's forgiveness for your sins by what you do with the Japanese Roses." Grant explained hoping to get inside of his head.

Harris laughed at Grant's comments, "The mighty Grant Dawson thinks he knows everything, but knows very little." Dan said. "Let me share a few of my secrets, maybe this time you will get the hint." He turned his back to Grant, "I kill to fix God's mistakes. And before these so-called innocents have judgment brought upon them, I make them confess their sins first. Afterward, I show the world who these people really are. As for the rose petals, they are used to show God himself that his mistakes have been rectified. To prove to him that he will always pay for not giving my daughter a second chance at life."

"You've gone mad!" Grant shouted. "The thing you hated the most is what you've become!"

"You still don't get." Dan laughed, "Grace understood, that's why I let her live. That way she could earn a second chance by doing God's work like me. You see it was supposed to be you that was going to join me, but you chased after your past. As much as it pained me I had to let you go. In the end, Grace served God well, and me, of course." Dan walked over to Grant and cut him loose. "It's time to end this." He walked over to the far end of the room and tossed Grant's gun over to him.

"What do you have in mind?"

"Just pick it up!" Harris demanded.

"Why?"

"Because if you don't, I will kill you. Now pick it up!" He held the gun up and aimed it right at Grant. It was clear that he wasn't playing games, he was going to kill the man before him if need be.

Grant was hesitant at first, though he did as he was told and retrieved the gun. "Don't do this, Dan! I don't want to kill you!" He shouted, trying to get through to his friend.

"Why not? Is this not what you do?" Harris looked like a man falling off the edge of a cliff with no way of saving himself.

"What drove you to this?!" He still refused to raise the gun.

"Why don't you ask the man that killed my daughter?" Dan replied. "Oh wait, you can't. The justice system decided to give the man a second chance, the man that killed my little girl! I fought against it, but was shut down! What choice did I have but to get my little girl the justice she deserves?! Then I watched all these other lowlives getting their second chance as well and I just couldn't have that happen.

I also used the people that would let me, like Grace and Leonard. Leonard was easy, he just wanted his cocaine. And it wasn't hard to get Grace's drunk mom to serve a purpose. But Grace's hatred for Mary ruined that and forced me to improvise, just like at the coroner's office. Though you know that, seeing how you found the keys I dropped by accident. But you can end this here and now."

"I'm not stupid," Grant said. "You're not going to use me as your fall guy the same way you used Grace."

"That's not what I had in mind." Harris smirked, "You were once a friend and a damn good cop. Join me, help me set things right or I'm going to have to kill you."

"I'm not going to help you kill people." He didn't want to kill Dan like he did the other criminals. They were pure evil, Harris didn't have that same feel to him. But it didn't seem he was going to give him a choice he would like.

"What if I said I would pay Mary a visit after I dealt with you?" Dan laughed like a crazed maniac. Hearing that set Grant off, he lifted the gun and aimed it at Dan. "That's more like it!" Harris lifted his gun again.

"Last chance to stop this madness!" Grant pleaded, though it was clear no words were going to get through to him.

"I can't let you interfere with things any longer."

"And I refuse to let you take more lives!"

Both men were getting ready to fire their weapons when a familiar voice called out, "Lower your gun, Dawson!" Grant turned his head to see Turner standing off to the side with his gun aimed at him.

"Can't do that, Turner." Grant responded. He finally realized that this man was beyond salvation. If Harris were allowed freedom he would start where he had left off.

"Do as I say!" Turner shouted.

"Looks like things didn't go the way you thought they would." Harris slyly grinned.

Grant looked around the room, that's when he noticed he was surrounded by cops, and all guns were on him. If he moved an inch or acted as though he might shoot the Captain. The cops would shoot him dead on the spot. Sweat formed above his brow, his hands nervously twitched. He could take Harris out now ending his reign of terror, but that would only sign his own death warrant.

"It's over, Dawson!" Turner shouted again.

This was not the way he was going to go out, he couldn't die, not here and not like this. Grant lowered the gun, and the cops closed in. Harris was all smiles, he truly thought he had fooled everyone. "Arrest that man!" He shouted. "Dawson is a cold blooded killer and I have all the proof I need. He's also connected with the disappearance of Captain Simons. I want him in handcuffs now!"

Grant found himself watching in bewilderment. The cops didn't close in on him but on Harris instead. "What is the meaning of this!" The Captain angrily shouted. "I am your commanding officer damn it! Arrest that man!"

"Enough of this Harris!" Turner hissed. "We already know it was you who killed all those people. It was you that kidnapped, Mary. And it was you that tried and failed to kill, Captain Simons. We can do this the easy way or the hard way. Just give me an excuse to use force."

Dan went to shoot Grant, if he was going down he would take as many with him that he could. One of the cops ended up knocking the gun from his hand. But he wasn't going to go quietly, Harris pulled a hunting knife from his robes. Stabbing one the cops in the throat, he quickly picked up his gun and shot two others. He turned and fired off a round at Turner, the bullet grazed his arm.

Grant lifted his gun returning fire, one of the bullets hit Harris's shoulder another his leg. The other officers in the room including Turner opened fire. It seemed like the gun fight lasted minutes, when it only lasted seconds. Dan managed to injure two more cops before he was taken down. As he laid there in a pool of his own blood, Grant walked up beside him. He looked down at the man with pity. This isn't the way he wanted things to end. Grant thought for sure he could save his old friend, but it was too late now. Evil had taken over Dan's everyday life, he had used and abused people. And this was his punishment for the sins he had committed.

"You're just as bad as me," Harris said looking up at Grant. He was coughing up blood but still alive. If he was able to survive, Grant felt like he would somehow get away with his crimes and be back out on the streets.

Dawson realized that his once friend couldn't be given that chance, "I only kill ones that I know are evil. You passed judgement and took it upon yourself to end lives that didn't deserve to be snuffed out. It's only a matter of time before things escalate." He raised the gun and pulled the trigger putting a bullet between his eyes. "Rest in peace old friend."

Tuner walked up beside Grant, "Pity Harris had fallen this far," he said with sadness.

"Can you blame him? His daughter was taken, and the system he believed in failed him. That could make anyone go mad."

"If we hadn't found Captain Simons, I doubt we would even have found this place. Or figured out that Dan was behind all this madness."

"She's alive?" Grant gasped.

"Yep," Turner said with a smile. "We found her hogtied in the basement of the police station barely alive. Harris had fought with her about dropping the midnight killer case. When she denied him, he knocked her out, and damn near beat her to death. I believe that she had found out about this place, was about to send a unit out to investigate. Until Harris decided he had to stop her."

"Glad to hear Simons survived," he responded. "Where are we anyway?"

"Baker's field."

"Where we trained as young cadets before they shut the place down." Grant had fond memories of the place.

"Nowhere better to hide your crimes," Turner said.

"Or the fact that no one can hear you scream when being tortured."

"Harris was a good man." Turner frowned. "Shame he couldn't be saved."

Grant didn't want to get sentimental, "There are times when you can't save a person," he said. "When I get back home I will send you my report."

"Leaving so soon?"

"Too much work to be done, I will have to leave as soon as possible."

"Sorry it turned out this way, Dawson," Turner said. "Still yet, thank you for all your help. I don't think this would have been solved without you." He stuck out his hand.

Grant reached out and shook Turner's hand, "If you ever need anything, don't call me." He laughed, "Just keep the people of Dover safe."

"I will," Turner said. "Oh and one more thing, please don't come back here again." He smirked and walked away.

Grant walked outside, he was definitely out in the middle of the woods A.K.A Baker's field. He was beginning to wonder just how in the hell he was going to get out of there. He wasn't about to ask Turner or any of the other cops for help. They had a mess to clean up and wounded men to tend to.

Then a certain car caught his attention, it was Harris's red seventy-nine mustang. Grant scanned the area, all eyes were on the crime scene and none on him. He casually walked over to the car and pulled on the door handle. The car door opened and he helped himself inside, he pulled down the sun visor and the keys fell into his lap.

"Nice," Grant smiled. He put the keys into the ignition and turned the key firing up the engine. It roared like thunder, he put the gear in drive, pushed the gas pedal with his foot and off the car went.

Later he showed up at Isaiah's house at around one o'clock in the morning, the loud engine of the car announced his return. Isaiah, Mary, and Tonya appeared on the porch, Isaiah with his trusty shotgun in hand. Grant got out of the vehicle, "Relax guys! It's just me!" He shouted.

Mary took off running towards him, once close enough she jumped into his arms. "Thank God you're safe," Mary whispered to him. "I was worried something bad had happened to you."

"Don't worry, I'm alright." He smiled and hugged her back.

Isaiah and Tonya walked down the porch steps joining Grant and Mary by the car. "So I take it the deed has been done?" Isaiah asked.

Grant nodded, "It has."

Mary looked up at him, "What is he talking about?" She asked.

"Hades has been dealt with," Grant told her. "You and everyone in Dover is safe now."

"Who was the man behind the mask?" Mary questioned. Grant glanced away, unsure of how to answer her question. "I see." She looked down at the ground. With the way he reacted was all the answer she needed.

"What will you do now?" Tonya asked.

"I have to head home," Grant replied. "Need to send my report to the Dover police, and the Mayor as well."

"Well if you ever need us you know where we will be," Tonya said. "Come on Isaiah, walk with me under the stars."

Isaiah slapped Grant on the shoulder, "You still owe me that favor." He chuckled. "Be careful out there my friend." He turned and took Tonya's hand in his and they walked away together into darkness.

"Are you leaving tonight?" Mary asked.

"I think it's for the best," Grant responded.

"Will you come back?"

"Not unless I'm needed. "What will you do now that this ordeal is over?"

She looked around stretching her arms high taking in the night air. "Tonya offered for me to stay with them for a while, I think I will take her up on that."

"And after that?" Grant questioned her. "Will you go back to work at the police station?"

"I don't think so. Dover is a place of good and bad memories for me, I think it's time I start over. After all that I have been through, I realized that I haven't done much with my life. And it's time to change that."

"Good." He smiled. "Change can be exciting. I wish you all the luck in the world."

"Thank you." She smiled in return. "I have you to thank for that." Mary went in for a long kiss. Embracing Grant for a long intimate moment, "I'm going to miss that. Remember, I love you and I always will." She ran her fingers down his cheek, "Don't lose yourself," Mary said to him as if more of a warning than anything else.

He cracked a faint smile, "Maybe we will see each other again someday." He bent over and kissed her cheek. "Take care of yourself," Grant whispered in her ear. "I love you too."

Grant and Mary stood there for several more seconds, sharing the last of the time they had left. He got back into the driver's seat of the Mustang, gave Mary one last smile before putting the car in reverse. Mary, with tears in her eyes refused to walk away until the tail lights of the car disappeared into the night.

THE
END

Dear reader,

We hope you enjoyed reading *The Ninth Precinct*. Please take a moment to leave a review, even if it's a short one. Your opinion is important to us.

Discover more books by A.E. Stanfill at https://www.nextchapter.pub/authors/ae-stanfill

Want to know when one of our books is free or discounted? Join the newsletter at http://eepurl.com/bqqB3H

Best regards,

A.E. Stanfill and the Next Chapter Team

Lightning Source UK Ltd.
Milton Keynes UK
UKHW040106010820
367514UK00009B/169